A JAINE AUSTEN MYSTERY

Shoes to Die For

LAURA LEVINE

𝑘

KENSINGTON BOOKS
KENSINGTON PUBLISHING CORP.
http://www.kensingtonbooks.com

KENSINGTON BOOKS are published by

Kensington Publishing Corp.
850 Third Avenue
New York, NY 10022

All Kensington titles, imprints and distributed lines are
available at special quantity discounts for bulk purchases
for sales promotion, premiums, fund-raising, educational
or institutional use.

Special book excerpts or customized printings can also
be created to fit specific needs. For details, write or phone
the office of the Kensington Special Sales Manager: Kensington Publishing Corp., 850 Third Avenue, New York,
NY 10022. Attn: Special Sales Department. Phone: 1-800-
221-2647.

Kensington and the K logo Reg. U.S. Pat. & TM Off.

ISBN 0-7582-0782-4

First Hardcover Printing: June 2005
First Mass Market Paperback Printing: May 2006
10 9 8 7 6 5 4 3 2 1

Printed in the United States of America

For Gracie,
and all the other treasured ladies
in my life.

Acknowledgments

Thanks to my editor extraordinaire, John Scogna-miglio, for coming up with such a nifty title and murder weapon. To my agent Evan Marshall, for always being there when I need him. To Joanne Fluke, author of the delicious Hannah Swensen mysteries, for her many acts of kindness and generosity. To Carlos Marrero, for yet another eye-catching cover. To my wonderful husband Mark, for putting up with me all year. And finally, thanks to my cat, Mr. Guy, because he refuses to get off my computer until I thank him.

Chapter 1

There are two kinds of people in L.A. Those who do lunch. And those who eat lunch. Those who do lunch talk to their agents and order things like ahi tuna and Chinese chicken salad. Those who eat lunch talk to a clown and order extra ketchup for their fries.

I am definitely one of the eat-lunchers, as anyone can tell from the impressive collection of fast food wrappers in my garbage can.

But on the day my story begins, I had broken ranks with my fellow slobs and was heading across town to do lunch with my neighbor Lance. It was warm and hazy, and as I drove east toward La Brea Avenue I could almost make out the Hollywood sign behind a curtain of smog.

La Brea Avenue is a hotbed of hipness in midtown Los Angeles. A onetime industrial street, it's now dotted with boutiques and restaurants so cool they don't bother with signs out front. And it was to one of those restaurants, a place called Café Ennui, that I was headed. Only I was having a hell of a time finding it.

I'd driven up and down the stretch between Wilshire and Melrose at least three times and was about to give

up when I saw a funky restaurant with a fifties diner
table in the window. This must be it, I thought, as I
parked my Corolla a few doors down. By now I was a
good fifteen minutes late. I dashed into the restaurant,
only to find that Lance wasn't there. I figured he was
tied up with a demanding customer. Lance is a salesman at Neiman Marcus, in the designer shoe department. Or as Lance likes to say, "I work in high heels."

I took a seat at the table in the window and glanced
around the restaurant. The place was an eclectic mix of
funky tables and chairs. I was surprised to see I was the
only customer.

A skinny guy with a shaved head stood behind a
counter and shot me an icy stare. Not exactly service
with a smile. I waved him over. Reluctantly, he got off his
stool and started across the room.

"Hi," I chirped, trying my best to ignore his look of
disdain. "Do you think I could see a menu?"

"Sweetie," he snipped, "this isn't a restaurant."

"It isn't?"

"No, it's a furniture store."

I looked around and for the first time noticed price
tags dangling from the tables and chairs.

"This isn't Café Ennui?"

"Nooo, it's not," he said slowly, as if talking to a
three-year-old.

"Then I guess you won't be getting a tip," I said,
with a feeble smile.

He was not amused.

"Café Ennui is over there."

He pointed a bony finger across the street to a store-
front with blackened windows. No wonder I'd missed
it. The place looked like it had gone out of business
decades ago.

I slid out of my chair and, under the withering glare

of my petulant furniture salesman, dashed across the street.

As it turns out, Café Ennui was anything but abandoned. Behind the blackened windows sat a gaggle of people who looked like they'd just stepped out of a Banana Republic ad, sipping mineral water and nibbling on various forms of lettuce. The average waistline hovered somewhere in the low twenties.

I looked around and spotted Lance. It was hard to miss him, with his headful of tight blond curls and lime green T-shirt. I hustled over to where he sat at a tiny table for two.

"Sorry I'm late," I said, plopping down into an uncomfortable metal chair, "but I couldn't find the place. Do you realize the sign out front is the size of a postage stamp?"

"I know. They try to keep it exclusive. Even their phone number is unlisted."

Welcome to La La Land, where colonic irrigation parlors take out full-page ads in the Yellow Pages, but restaurants are unlisted.

Lance shot me a disapproving look.

"Jaine, honey. Do you realize you're the only person in the restaurant wearing elastic-waist pants?"

He was right, of course. The place was filled with perfect bodies in low-rider jeans and tank tops, slender midriffs exposed. And those were just the guys.

"So what?" I said, reaching for the menu. "Am I going to be arrested by the pants police?"

He shook his head and sighed.

I sighed, too, when I checked out the menu. What a disaster. All I saw was arugula and radicchio and baby vegetables. Not a calorie in sight. The most interesting thing on the menu was an old coffee stain.

Just when I was wondering if I could possibly convince Lance to ditch this place for a restaurant that served actual food, a sultry waitress with huge eyes and tiny boobs slithered up to us.

"What can I get you today?" she asked, with a brittle smile.

"How about something from McDonald's?"

No, I didn't really say that. What I said was: "Got any burgers?"

"We've got the ahi tuna burger with carmelized fennel."

"Sounds mighty tempting, but I'll pass."

There was no way out of it. I'd have to order a salad.

"I'll have the turkey cobb."

"Free-range turkey or regular?" asked Ms. Sultry.

"Regular's okay."

"What kind of dressing? Raspberry vinaigrette, balsamic vinaigrette, or kiwi vinaigrette?"

"Surprise me," I said, throwing caution to the wind.

Ms. Sultry, who looked like her last lunch had been a line of cocaine, took Lance's order and slinked away.

"Really, Jaine," Lance said, eyeing my *Dukakis for President* T-shirt. "You're so hopelessly out of date. Don't you want to be hip?"

"I'll settle for hippy."

"Oh, c'mon. You're not nearly the chubbette you think you are."

"In a town where a six is considered a plus size, I'm a chubbette."

"You happen to be a very attractive woman. All you need is a little fashion advice." Then, as if he'd just thought of it, he said, "Hey, that's not a bad idea. How about I give you a fashion makeover?"

And then it dawned on me. I knew what this was all about.

"You're looking for a project, aren't you? You're

bored and lonely and between boyfriends, and you want something to do."

"That's not true!"

But of course it was true. Ever since Lance discovered his last boyfriend was a married man, he'd been sulking around his apartment like a teenager with a rusted nipple ring.

I shot him a wilting look.

"Okay, so maybe it is true," he confessed. "Maybe I am looking for a project. But that doesn't change the fact that you're in desperate need of a makeover."

"Forget it, Lance. If God wanted me to wear low-rider jeans, he would've never invented fudge ripple ice cream."

At which point, our waitress slithered back to our table with our lunches. We spent the rest of our meal trying to find actual food among our lettuce, and talking about what a rat Lance's ex-boyfriend was. Every once in a while, Lance sneaked a peek at the guys in the room, while I sneaked a peek at the dessert menu. Nothing too exciting there. Just some nonfat sorbet, amaretto biscotti, and a flourless carrot cake. Lance and I shared the carrot cake, a tiny square of orange sludge with a sprig of mint on top.

We paid our bill and headed out into the hazy sunshine.

"Let's go for a walk," Lance said, "and burn off some calories."

"What calories? There weren't enough calories on that menu to feed an anorexic gnat."

"Come on," he said, grabbing my arm. "We could both use the exercise."

So we strolled up the street, past one terminally trendy boutique after another.

"Look!" Lance said, stopping suddenly in front of a

unisex clothing store. "Passions. My favorite clothing store. A friend of mine works here. Let's stop in and say hi."

But that whole surprise act wasn't fooling me.

"We didn't just happen to walk by this place, did we?" I said. "You had this all planned as part of your fashion makeover."

"Okay," Lance admitted, "so I had it planned. But I still want to say hi to my friend. Are you coming with me or not?'

Like a fool, I said yes.

And that's how all the trouble started.

Chapter 2

Passions was an uber-hip joint with gleaming hard-wood floors, pulsating rock music, and fashions cut so small, for a minute I thought I was in a children's clothing store.

Lance's friend turned out to be a pixie in her twenties with Day-Glo orange hair that looked like it was styled with an eggbeater. Together with her big blue eyes and itsy-bitsy figure, she just about broke the needle on the cute-o-meter.

"Becky and I used to work together at Neiman's," Lance said, after he'd introduced us.

Somehow I couldn't picture this elf, with her flaming hair and earrings the size of hula hoops, in the refined sales aisles of Neiman Marcus.

"My hair wasn't orange back then," she said, as if reading my mind. "I worked in ladies lingerie. Frankly it was a bit of a snore. It's so much more fun here. I even get to do the windows."

I glanced over at the window display, featuring a mannequin in thigh-high boots and thong underwear. Just what I always wanted. The sexy storm trooper look.

I picked up a tank top the size of a handkerchief.

"Just out of curiosity," I asked, "do you have anything in a size large?"

"That *is* a size large."

I rolled my eyes in disbelief.

"Jaine's a writer," Lance said. "She's not really into the fashion scene."

"A writer?" Becky asked, clearly impressed.

I nodded modestly.

And it's true. I write resumes, personals ads, and industrial brochures. Perhaps you've read my blockbuster brochure for Toiletmasters Plumbers (*In a Rush to Flush? Call Toiletmasters.*)

"I adore writers!" Becky gushed. She blinked those big blue eyes of hers, and I couldn't help wondering if she'd actually ever read a book.

"Tyler's a writer, too." She pointed to a salesman helping a customer in the men's section. "He's writing a novel."

Lance eyed him with interest. And for good reason. Tyler was one eminently eyeable guy. Tall and slim, with an innocent face and a killer body, he managed to look both sweet and sexy at the same time.

"Forget it, Lance," Becky said, following his hungry look. "He's straight."

"Are you sure about that? I don't mind a challenge."

"I'm sure, Lance. In fact, he used to date Frenchie."

"Frenchie?"

"The blonde at the counter. Her real name is Giselle but everybody calls her Frenchie."

We followed her gaze to a brittle blonde sitting at a stool in front of the register, talking into her cell phone. Her white-blond hair, pulled into a tight bun, contrasted sharply with her blood-red lipstick and fingernails. She wore a low-cut black dress and ridiculously high stiletto heels, which she tapped impatiently as she talked. Nestled in her cleavage was a gold Maltese cross. Yet somehow I didn't figure her for much of a churchgoer.

"Where the hell is my pizza?" she shrieked. "I've been waiting over an hour!"

Her name may have been French, but her accent was strictly Brooklyn.

"A cutie like Tyler dated her?" Lance's eyes were wide with disbelief. "Quelle bitch."

"You know who she's talking to on the phone?" Becky said.

"An unlucky pizza parlor?"

"Her husband. She bosses him around like a trained seal."

"Don't forget to pick up my dry cleaning," Frenchie barked, before slamming down the phone.

"Wait a minute," Lance said. "She dated Tyler, and she's married?"

Becky rolled her eyes. "You wouldn't believe how much she cheats on her husband. I'm surprised she hasn't hit on the UPS man yet."

Lance shook his head, baffled. "What was a cutie like Tyler doing with a bitch like her?"

"Oh, Frenchie can be charming when she wants to be. But eventually Tyler realized how awful she was and dumped her."

"I wish you wouldn't say nasty things about Frenchie."

I turned around to see a mousy woman in a tweed suit and sensible low-heeled pumps. Her brown hair formed a frizzy halo around her head. She looked as out of place in this joint as I did.

"Frenchie is a very nice person when you get to know her," the mouse said reprovingly, then scurried away toward the back of the store.

"That's Maxine, the bookkeeper," Becky said. "Poor thing. She's got a mad crush on Frenchie. Frenchie barely gives her the time of day, but Maxine still worships her."

"Hello, Frenchie," Maxine said, waving shyly as she passed Frenchie.

Frenchie gave her a faint smile and went back to examining her cuticles. Then the phone rang, and she answered it.

"Passions," she said, dropping her voice an octave, like a phone sex operator. "How may I help you?" Suddenly, she was back to her Brooklyn roots. "Oh, for crying out loud, Owen! You're still stuck in traffic? Just get here already; I'm starving."

She slammed down the phone, her face clouded in anger. But in the very next instant the storm clouds disappeared and her face was wreathed in smiles.

"Mrs. Tucker!" she said, jumping off her stool and heading to the front door to greet a customer, clomping along in those ridiculous high heels of hers.

"Jimmy Choo knockoffs," Lance said, following my gaze.

"Who's Jimmy Choo?" I asked.

"Send this girl to fashion camp," Lance said, rolling his eyes. "He's only one of the world's hottest shoe designers."

Okay, so sue me if I happen to shop at Payless.

By now Frenchie was at the door, air-kissing her customer.

"How nice to see you, Mrs. Tucker," she cooed.

"Mrs. Tucker's one of our best customers," Becky whispered. "Frenchie never lets her out of her sight."

Mrs. Tucker was a woman in her fifties who dressed like a kid in her twenties. There was something creepy about the way she'd crammed her menopausal body into low-rider jeans and a midriff-baring tee. I'm no fashion expert, but I think its safe to say you should stop baring your midriff once it's got liver spots.

"Love your outfit," Frenchie gushed.

"You should, sweetie," the older woman said. "You sold it to me."

Frenchie laughed gaily. "So what can I show you today? We've got some fabulous new capri's that'll look just smashing on you."

Like a blond hurricane, she swept through the racks, pulling out one item of clothing after the next. Mrs. Tucker's eyes shone with anticipation. After Frenchie got her set up in a dressing room, she hurried over to where we were standing.

"What a silly old bat," she said. "If I had a tummy as pouchy as hers, I'd shoot myself.

"Where the hell is the label thingie?" she asked, rummaging in a drawer behind the counter.

"It's right here," Becky said, handing her a device that looked like a stapler.

"Just watch," Frenchie said, ripping out the size 8 label from a pair of sequinned capri's. "She's going to ask for these in a size 6. You'll see."

And as if on cue, Mrs. Tucker popped her head out the dressing room door.

"Frenchie, honey. These are a size 8. You know I wear a size 6."

"Right, Mrs. Tucker," Frenchie said. "I'll go find you a pair."

As soon as Mrs. Tucker disappeared back into the dressing room, Frenchie looked through the drawer and found a size 6 label. In an instant, thanks to the "label thingie," Frenchie had it sewn onto the capri's.

"Here we go, Mrs. Tucker," she trilled, heading for the dressing room. "A size 6."

"Did I just see what I think I saw?" I asked, amazed.

"Yes," Becky said. "We switch size labels all the time."

"What a brilliant idea. I wish Bloomingdale's would start doing that. If they did, I might even try on a bathing suit."

"As long as we're here," Lance said, "why don't you try on a few outfits?"

"I already told you. I'm not interested in buying any clothes."

"Oh, come on. Just one outfit."

"No way, Lance. I'm not trying anything on. Nada. Zilch. Nothing."

Ten minutes later I was squeezed into a dressing room with an outrageous assortment of outfits I'd never in a million years dream of wearing. There were skintight pants, see-through blouses, and one of those handkerchief-sized tank tops I'd seen earlier.

"How am I supposed to get into this?" I asked, waving it out the dressing room door.

"It's spandex," Lance said. "It stretches."

Somehow I managed to squeeze myself into it. And for the first time in my life I knew what it felt like to be a sausage.

"Try it on with the harem pants," Becky called out.

Oh, God. Those harem pants. Just the memory of them makes me shudder. I'll spare you the gruesome details. Let's just say I looked like Barbara Eden on prednisone.

I stepped out of the dressing room and everyone gasped. Not in admiration, I can assure you.

From over at the counter, where Mrs. Tucker was

paying for her "size 6" pants, Frenchie didn't even bother to stifle a laugh.

I struggled through a few more outfits, each one more disastrous than the last.

Eventually even Lance gave up.

"I think Jaine's more the tailored type," Becky said diplomatically.

I scrambled back into my elastic-waist pants and T-shirt and came back out of the dressing room, ready to strangle Lance for putting me through such a humiliating ordeal.

Perhaps sensing how irritated I was, and trying to make amends, Becky said: "Hey, Jaine. I was just wondering. Have you ever written any advertising copy?"

I nodded. Of course, not everyone would consider Toiletmasters a major account, but it *was* advertising.

"It just so happens that the owner of the store is looking for someone to write a new ad campaign. Would you be interested in the job?"

Suddenly I was in a much better mood. Paychecks have a way of doing that to me.

"Should I try to set up an interview for you?" Becky asked.

And, in another move I'd live to regret, I said yes.

Chapter 3

I drove home on Cloud Nine.

Well, technically I drove home on Olympic Boulevard, which was clogged with bumper-to-bumper traffic. But I didn't care. I had an actual job prospect. Something I desperately needed. You see, I'd just lost one of my biggest clients, Tip Top Dry Cleaners. They'd decided to go with a full-service advertising agency, instead of a woman in sweat pants cranking out ads at her dining room table. Well, phooey on them. I sincerely doubt any ad agency could match my slogan. (*At Tip Top Cleaners, We Clean for You, We Press for You, We Even Dye for You.*)

But the fact remained, I had a pesky little thing called rent to pay, and so any job offer was a welcome one. So what if I didn't know the first thing about funky fashions? So what if, aside from belly buttons, I had no idea what was "in" or "out"? I bet plenty of great ad campaigns were created by people who didn't know much about the product they were selling. For all I knew, the guy who invented *Got Milk?* was lactose intolerant.

The first thing I saw when I let myself into my apartment was my cat, Prozac, hard at work at my computer. Okay, so she wasn't writing. She was licking her privates. But she was working hard at it.

"Hi, poopsie," I crooned. "How's my little love bug?"

My little love bug yawned and went back to her G spot.

One of these days, I'm going to get myself a sweet slobbering dog who'll cover me with wet kisses the minute I walk in the front door. But until then, Prozac is my only significant other. We share a one-bedroom apartment in a 1940s duplex in the slums of Beverly Hills, far from the megamansions north of Sunset. Not that I'm complaining. I happen to love our apartment. It's on a pretty tree-lined block, right up the street from a Starbucks. We've got hardwood floors, original tile in the bathroom, and a great view of our neighbor's azalea bush. The only thing I don't like about it is the aforementioned rent, which has the annoying habit of coming due at the beginning of each month.

Still starving after the three shards of lettuce I'd had for lunch, I fixed myself a healthy snack of peanut butter and Pop Tarts. Then I scooped Prozac off my keyboard and spent the rest of the afternoon working on a resume for one of my clients, a recent LSU graduate. (The LSU in this case standing for Lazy, Slow, and Unskilled.) It wasn't easy thinking up accolades for a kid who seemed destined to spend the rest of his life asking, "Would you like fries with that?"

Eventually, Prozac woke up from her umpteenth nap of the day and began howling for her dinner. I fixed her a bowl of Fancy Fish Guts and grabbed a light dinner of Cheerios and bananas for myself. Of course, I use the term "light" advisedly. At Café Ennui, it probably would have fed a family of four.

I always try to eat light the night of my class.

Once a week I teach memoir writing at the Shalom Retirement Home. There's not much teaching involved. Mainly, it's listening. Each week my students, mostly women in their eighties, show up, health permitting, with their treasured memories. Most of their essays are scratched out on old-fashioned lined paper. Only Mrs. Horowitz has a computer, a laptop her son bought her, which she confesses she uses as a plant stand. Their stories aren't written with the greatest of skill, but they are written from the heart, and I consider it a privilege to hear them.

The only fly in the Shalom ointment is Abe Goldman. The lone man in my class, Mr. Goldman is an argumentative old coot who bears an uncanny resemblance to Mr. Magoo. Just my luck, he's madly in love with me.

That night when I showed up at Shalom I found a box of Tic Tacs at my spot at the head of the table.

"For you, cookie," Mr. Goldman said with a wink. Or maybe it was a blink. Mr. Goldman has an unfortunate tic so I can never tell whether he's winking or blinking.

"Thank you," I said, smiling weakly.

"To make your breath kissing sweet," he added, with another wink/blink.

"So," I said, deftly changing the subject. "Who wants to read their essay?"

Mr. Goldman's hand shot up like a piston. Mr. Goldman was always eager to read another chapter in the saga of his life as a carpet salesman.

I looked around the room, desperate for another volunteer. But my ladies, unlike Mr. Goldman, were often shy about reading their essays, especially the first essay of the evening, before the literary ice had been broken.

"Anyone?" I called out, ignoring Mr. Goldman's hand, now waving frantically.

I shot a pleading look at Mrs. Pechter, a round powder puff of a woman with bosoms as big as throw pillows, but she just popped a Tootsie Roll in her mouth. I switched my imploring gaze to her best friend, Mrs. Rubin, but she shook her head no.

Finally Mrs. Horowitz, she of the plant stand computer, raised her hand.

"Mrs. Horowitz! Thank goodness. I thought we'd have to listen to Mr. Goldman yammer on about the joys of broadloom for the next twenty minutes."

Okay, so I didn't really say that. What I said was, "Go right ahead, Mrs. H."

Mrs. Horowitz was an imposing woman with steel gray hair and a purse the size of an overnight bag. She fished out her essay from the depths of her purse, then took a deep breath and began:

"A Day at the Boardwalk."

Mrs. Horowitz wrote about going to Coney Island with her parents as a child—riding the steamy IRT subway from Flatbush to Brighton Beach, eating hot dogs with pickle relish, wearing long one-piece bathing suits, and teasing her father, who never ventured out from the shade of their beach umbrella.

As Shalom essays went, it was excellent. Lots of interesting details and, like most of my students' efforts, written from the heart.

"Very good!" I said when she was through. "Any comments, class?"

"Wonderful," said Mrs. Pechter.

"I liked it, too," said Mrs. Rubin. A tiny birdlike woman who played Robin to Mrs. Pechter's Batman, Mrs. Rubin often echoed her best friend's sentiments.

Mrs. Greenberg and Mrs. Zahler chimed in with their praises.

Only Mr. Goldman looked unenthused.

"It was the BMT," he said.

"What?" Mrs. Horowitz blinked, puzzled.

"It wasn't the IRT subway," Mr. Goldman said. "It was the BMT that went from Flatbush to Brighton Beach."

"Mr. Goldman," I said, "we're talking about the quality of writing. About imagery and feelings. What does it matter if it's the IRT or the BMT?"

"It matters plenty if you want to get to Brighton Beach."

I fought back the impulse to hurl a Tic Tac at him.

Mrs. Horowitz's eyes blazed with fire.

"Don't tell me it was the BMT, Abe. It was the IRT."

"BMT."

"You're saying my memory's no good?"

"That's exactly what I'm saying."

"Look who's talking," Mrs. Pechter piped up. "The man who forgets to zip up his fly."

"I never forget to zip up!" Mr. Goldman shot back. "Sometimes I forget to zip down, maybe, but never up!"

"If Mrs. Horowitz said she rode the IRT," Mrs. Zahler chimed in, "she rode the IRT."

"Not to Brighton Beach, she didn't."

"I loved Mrs. Horowitz's description of eating that hot dog with relish," I said, eager to put an end to the subway debate.

"Feh," said Mr. Goldman. "I don't like hot dogs with relish. I like mine with sauerkraut."

"Wonderful job, Mrs. Horowitz," I said, ignoring Mr. Goldman's culinary preferences. "Now who'd like to read next?"

Mrs. Zahler and Mrs. Rubin read their essays, and then—with a half hour to go before the end of the class—I could no longer ignore Mr. Goldman's hand, waving frantically in my face.

"Mr. Goldman," I said, with a forced smile. "What've you got?"

My eyes glazed over as Mr. Goldman started reading his latest installment in the story of his life as a carpet salesman. This time he wrote about going to see Debbie Reynolds' show at a carpet sellers' convention in Las Vegas. I can't remember the details because, frankly, I wasn't listening. Instead I was deciding which flavor of ice cream to pick up on the way home from class. I was debating between Chunky Monkey and Rocky Road when something Mr. Goldman said caught my attention:

And then after the show, Debbie Reynolds said to me, "So, Abe, how about coming up to my hotel room for a little hanky-panky?"

Inwardly I groaned. In Mr. Goldman's memoirs, every attractive woman he met had the hots for him.

Modesty forbids me to divulge the details of what happened next, Mr. Goldman went on, *but let's just say that when Debbie gave me her autographed picture, she wrote, "To Abe Goldman, I'll never forget our night of bliss in the jacuzzi. Yours very sincerely, Debbie Reynolds."*

Mrs. Pechter snorted with derision. "You and Debbie Reynolds? Don't make me laugh."

"Now look who's getting the facts wrong," Mrs. Rubin chimed in.

"This isn't a fiction course," Mrs. Horowitz said with a sneer. "You're supposed to write the truth."

"That is the truth," Mr. Goldman insisted.

"Are you sure you're not taking a little poetic license?" I asked.

"No, I'm not taking poetic license. It really happened!"

"I don't believe it!" Mrs. Horowitz snapped.

"What do you know?" Mr. Goldman said. "You think the IRT stops at Brighton Beach."

"Well, class, I see our time is up for tonight."

"No, it's not," Mr. Goldman said, checking his watch. "We still got ten minutes to go."

"Time's up," I repeated in the steeliest voice I could muster.

The ladies gathered their purses and back support cushions and headed out into the hallway. Only Mr. Goldman lingered behind.

"So, cookie," he said with a wink/blink. "Want to go for a moonlight stroll in the parking lot?"

Not in this lifetime, I didn't.

"Sorry, Mr. Goldman. I can't. Why don't you give Debbie Reynolds a call?"

Okay, so I didn't make the crack about Debbie Reynolds. I just grabbed my Tic Tacs and ran.

I made a pit stop at the market to pick up some ice cream and came home to find Prozac still curled up on my keyboard. I scooped her off and checked my e-mails. Just a message from someone named Heidi who had pictures of hot girls with barnyard animals she wanted to share with me. And some letters from my parents.

After an evening doing battle with Mr. Goldman, I didn't have the strength to deal with my parents. Don't get me wrong. My parents are lovely people. But high maintenance. The two of them attract trouble like sofa bottoms attract dust bunnies. Everything in their lives somehow evolves into high drama. Drama that worries me half to death, yet manages to leave them unscarred.

To paraphrase the late, great Henny Youngman, my parents don't have ulcers. They're just carriers. No, I'd wait to read their letters in the morning.

In the meanwhile, I got undressed and headed for the tub, where I spent the next half hour up to my neck in steamy water. Just me, my rubber duckie, and my good buddies Ben & Jerry.

YOU'VE GOT MAIL

To: Jausten
From: Shoptillyoudrop
Subject: Big News

Hi, darling—

Keep your eye out for the UPS man. I just sent you the most fabulous cubic zirconia engagement ring from The Shopping Channel. Two carats, set in platinum over sterling silver. It was on sale, only $39.95, plus shipping and handling. And before you go jumping down my throat, yes, I know that technically you're not engaged, but you can always wear it on your right hand as a cocktail ring. And besides, a mother can dream, can't she?

Big news here at Tampa Vistas. We have a new social director, a genuine Broadway writer and actor. Everyone's very excited. His name is Alistair St. Germaine. Maybe you've heard of him? He's done all sorts of plays, mainly Off Broadway. Not only that, he used to be a brain surgeon, too. Although it seems strange, doesn't it, him being a writer and an actor *and* a brain surgeon? Anyhow, he's written a play that he's going to produce right here in our clubhouse. Daddy is going to audition for the lead. Isn't that exciting?

Well, keep your eye out for that engagement ring. And for a fiancé to go with it, haha!

Lots of love,
Mom

To: Jausten
From: DaddyO
Subject: Your Daddy, the Actor

Hi, honeybunch—I guess Mom has told you the big
news. I'm going to be starring in a play at the Tampa
Vistas clubhouse. We've got a new social director, some
hotshot writer from New York, a real smart guy; I can
just tell he's oozing with talent.

He's written a hilarious British drawing room comedy,
sort of like Noël Coward used to write, called *Lord
Worthington's Ascot.*

I'm going to play Lord Worthington. I haven't actually
gotten the part yet, but it's a shoo-in. Most of the old
farts here can't remember their middle names, let alone
thirty pages of dialogue.

Besides, I've had lots of theatrical experience. Did I
ever tell you I starred in my high school production of
Romeo and Juliet? The local paper came to review it
and said, "Hank Austen was more than adequate as
Romeo." I've got the clipping in a scrapbook somewhere.

If I do say so myself, I've got a real flair for this sort
of thing. Well, I've got to get busy and learn my lines.

Hope all is well in sunny California.

Your loving,
Daddy

To: Jausten
From: Shoptillyoudrop
Subject: P.S.

P.S. I was wrong about Mr. St. Germaine. He wasn't a brain surgeon. He just played one on TV.

Chapter 4

I woke up the next morning to the sweet sounds of Prozac howling for her breakfast. After sloshing some Fancy Mackerel Innards into her bowl, I did my usual fifty sit-ups and fixed myself a continental breakfast of fresh brewed coffee and croissants. Okay, I didn't do any sit-ups. The only exercise I got was brushing my teeth. And my breakfast was instant coffee and a Pop Tart. Okay, two Pop Tarts.

Then I hunkered down at the computer to read my parents' e-mails.

So Mom had sent me yet another piece of jewelry from the shopping channel. That's one thing you should know about my mother: She's a TV shopaholic. In fact, she actually convinced my father to retire down to Tampa, Florida, so she could be near the Home Shopping Network. She claims this way she gets her packages sooner. I tried to explain that the stuff isn't actually shipped out from the TV studio, but she insisted on moving there anyway.

My mom has enough CZs to open her own zirconia mine. Most of them are gaudy rocks the size of Tootsie Pops. Every once in a while she decides to send me one.

Usually I just toss them in my underwear drawer and hope they'll morph into ladder-free pantyhose. But she means well.

Of course, I could do without her sledgehammer hints about getting married. I tried matrimony once and found it about as satisfying as athlete's foot.

I call my ex-husband The Blob. Mainly because Dostoyevsky already has first dibs on *The Idiot*. It's all too depressing to talk about. Let's just say The Blob was the kind of guy who was intimately acquainted with his own ear wax.

As for Daddy having the acting bug, I wasn't the least bit surprised. Daddy's always been a bit of a ham. When I was a kid he used to act out all my bedtime stories. For years, I thought Cinderella smoked a cigar.

My thoughts of Daddy's theatrical ambitions were interrupted by the phone ringing. I picked it up and a childlike voice chirped:

"Hi! It's me, Becky!"

The voice sounded so young, for a minute, I thought it was a wrong number, some high school kid calling her girlfriend to meet her at the mall.

"We met yesterday, at Passions," she said.

Right. The orange-haired angel who was going to get me a job interview.

"I spoke with Grace, the lady who owns the store, and she said she'd be happy to meet with you."

"That's wonderful. Thanks so much."

"Can you make it tomorrow morning at ten?"

After assuring her I could make it at ten, I hung up and turned to Prozac.

"Guess what! I have a job interview!"

"Congratulations!"

No, that wasn't Prozac talking. She's a clever cat but

she hasn't mastered the art of speech yet. That was Lance, standing outside my screen door.

"Becky just called me," he said, when I let him in. "Now the first thing we need to do is get you something to wear."

"Lance, I've got plenty to wear."

"I'll be the judge of that," he said, making a beeline for my bedroom closet.

"Oh, my God," he wailed, holding up a perfectly lovely tweed blazer. "When did you buy this? In the Carter administration?

"And who designed this?" He plucked a striped blouse from the closet and held it between two fingers like a dead mouse.

"I got it at a flea market. The label's missing but the saleslady swore it was Ralph Lauren."

"Looks more like Ralph Kramden to me."

"Very amusing."

"Listen, Jaine. You're always complaining about not having enough work. Did it ever occur to you that one of the reasons why you're not working as much as you'd like is your image?"

I hated to admit it, but maybe he had a point.

"This stuff may wow them at Toiletmasters," he said, waving at the contents of my closet, "but Grace Lynbrook is a different story. You know who she is, of course?"

I shook my head.

"Grace was one of the top fashion models back in the seventies. The woman has spent her whole life around designer clothes. I hate to break it to you, kiddo, but she's not going to be impressed with your cotton/poly blends."

"But I can't wear that crazy stuff she stocks in her

shop," I said, shuddering at the memory of those clown pants. "You saw how silly I looked."

"No," he agreed, "you have to go the classic route. Simple, elegant, clean lines, reeking of money. Make her think you don't need the job. That's when people want you. When they think you don't need them. Now get dressed. We're going shopping."

A half hour later, I found myself in a dressing room at Barneys trying on a $3,000 Prada suit. It was an icy-gray cashmere, soft as a baby's bottom. I stepped out of the dressing room and modeled it for Lance.

"Very nice," he said, nodding his approval.

I looked darn good, if I do say so myself. Those clean Prada lines took ten pounds off my body, many of them in the dreaded hip/tush zone.

"Didn't I tell you you'd look marvelous?" Lance beamed.

Suddenly I had a vision of a whole new me. A cool, elegant me, lunching at Spago, doing deals at Paramount, coming home to my Wilshire Boulevard penthouse, where I'd fix myself cosmopolitans at my imported marble wet bar. Unfortunately, the bubble burst when I pictured me getting the bill from Barneys.

"Lance, there's no way I can afford this suit."

"You don't have to buy it, silly. Just borrow it."

"What do you mean?"

"Put it on your credit card, wear it to the interview, and then return it."

"I can't do that."

"Of course you can. People do it all the time. I get shoes returned at Neiman's that have been worn to the Himalayas and back."

"You really think it's okay?"

"Absolutely!"

I wish I could tell you that there was a tiny voice inside me telling me not to do it, that it was morally wrong and unfair to Barneys. But the only voice I heard at the time was the one that was shouting, *You look ten pounds thinner!*

Which is why, with my checking account practically on life support, I found myself charging a $3,000 Prada suit on my Visa card.

It made perfect sense at the time.

"We've got to do something about your hair," Lance announced as we got on the elevator and headed down to Barneys' parking lot.

"What's wrong with my hair?"

"Nothing, if you don't mind looking like Shirley Temple on the *Good Ship Lollipop*."

Two of our elevator-mates—rail-thin girls with waists the size of my ankles—looked over at my curly mop and stifled giggles.

"Curly hair happens to be very stylish," I sniffed.

"It's not your curls that are the problem. It's your cut. Looks like someone went at you with a chainsaw."

More giggles from the anorexics. I hoped they choked on their diuretics.

"Oh, Jaine, don't pout," Lance said. I'm just telling you all this because I care about you."

The elevator stopped at our floor.

"Now come on," he said, taking me by the hand. "We're going to make you beautiful!"

Lance wove his tiny red Mini Cooper in and out of traffic until we reached our destination: a chi-chi hair salon in Brentwood called Gunter's.

"Gunter and I are good buddies," he said, as we strolled into the salon.

"Lance, sweetie!"

A tall, tanned blond guy came drifting toward us. So gorgeous, he practically took my breath away. Think Norse god, with a blow dryer.

The two of them embraced like old lovers, which I later found out they were.

"Let's see what you've brought me," he said, turning his gaze to me.

He stared at me from the left and from the right. From the back, and from the front. All the while shaking his head and tsk-tsking.

"Don't worry," he said, when he finally stopped circling. "They call me The Miracle Worker."

He snapped his fingers, and out of nowhere, a shampoo girl appeared. After a luxurious lathering and a lecture about the dangers of drugstore shampoo, I was led back to Gunter, who was waiting for me with his scissors at the ready. With lightning speed, he snipped away at my curls, until a thick blanket of discarded hair lay at his feet. Then he whipped out his dryer, and before my incredulous eyes, smoothed my hair into a soft, silky bob. Never had my hair looked so good.

Gunter was right. He was a miracle worker.

I didn't even mind the hundred dollars he charged for the miracle. Okay, I did mind, but as Lance said, it was investment grooming.

Still, I thought, as I wrote out a check that I prayed wouldn't bounce, I damn well better get that job.

"My God, you look gorgeous!"

I was sitting across from my best friend, Kandi

Tobolowsky, in Paco's Tacos, our favorite Mexican restaurant. She'd been oohing and aahing over my new look from the moment I walked in the door. She couldn't take her eyes off me. And she wasn't the only one. I saw our waiter staring at me, too. Although I suspect he was staring at the glob of guacamole I'd spilled on my blouse.

"You've got to give me Gunter's number," Kandi said. "Was he expensive?"

"Very."

Unlike me, Kandi can afford to go to Gunter. Kandi's a writer on *Beanie & the Cockroach,* a Saturday morning cartoon about a short-order cook named Beanie and his pet cockroach, Fred.

Now you probably assume that people who write dialogue for a cockroach don't get paid much. Well, you assume wrong. In the Life Isn't Fair Department, they get paid obscene amounts of money. A trip to Gunter's would barely make a dent in Kandi's checkbook.

Of course, Kandi didn't really need Gunter. Not as much as I did. Kandi's hair is enviably straight and glossy brown. The kind of fabulous hair you see models tossing in shampoo commercials.

"It's so exciting," Kandi said, taking a dainty bite of her chip, "about your job interview tomorrow. Although I still can't quite picture you writing about fashion. Whatever you do, don't wear elastic-waist pants!"

"No elastic-waist pants," I promised.

"And no T-shirts with silly sayings."

"Of course I won't wear a T-shirt."

Frankly I was getting a little miffed at the way everybody seemed to assume I was a fashion dummy.

"I know what to wear to an interview," I said, with more than a little iciness in my voice.

"What? What are you wearing?"

"A suit."

"What kind of suit?"

I must've been feeling guilty about my scheme to "borrow" the Prada suit, because I said brusquely, "It's a perfectly nice suit. Now can we talk about something other than my clothes?"

"Okay," Kandi said. "What about your eyebrows? You think you might do a little tweezer action, or are you going to stick with the Andy Rooney look?"

"Kandi!"

"Oh, don't get all pissy. I just thought your eyebrows could use a little shaping."

At which point our waiter showed up to take our dinner order.

"More guacamole?" he asked, eyeing the stain on my blouse.

"No, we don't need any more guacamole," Kandi piped up.

We both ordered a sensible dinner of chicken tacos and salad, hold the rice and beans. Okay, so I didn't hold the rice and beans. And I ordered a beef burrito instead of a taco. Which is why I happen to be so fond of those elastic-waist pants that send Kandi and Lance into cardiac arrest.

"Guess what, honey?" Kandi said, when our waiter had gone. "I've discovered a fab new way to meet guys."

Kandi's always trying to drag me, kicking and screaming, into the wonderful world of dating. She can't seem to get it through her head that just the thought of a date makes me break out in a cold sweat. Kandi, on the other hand, has a black belt in dating. For some inexplicable reason, she finds the whole process fun.

"Don't you want me to tell you the fab way to meet guys?" she asked.

"Not really."

"Speed dating!" she plowed ahead anyway. "You know, where you get to meet twenty guys in just one evening."

"Kandi, I'm not interested in meeting one guy, let alone twenty."

She shook her head and sighed.

"Jaine, honey, just because you had one disastrous marriage, that's no reason to hole yourself up with a passive-aggressive cat for the rest of your life."

"Prozac is not passive-aggressive," I huffed. "She's just a little bossy, that's all."

"One of the producers at *Beanie* tried speed dating," Kandi said, unswayed from her mission. "She met three guys! All really nice."

"Sorry, Kandi. I'm not interested."

"But I already signed you up."

"Unsign me."

"I can't. I already paid, and there are no refunds."

We argued about it all through dinner, until our waiter brought out a lovely flan for dessert and I finally gave in.

"Okay," I sighed. "I'll go."

I only agreed to do it because I was feeling guilty about the money Kandi had laid out. That, and because she refused to give me my dessert fork until I said yes.

Chapter 5

I didn't get much sleep that night. I spent most of the wee hours lying stiffly on my back, trying not to mess up my hair. Finally I managed to doze off, but I guess I must've tossed and turned because I woke up the next morning with a cowlick the size of a small boomerang. Oh, well, I'd batten it down somehow.

But first, I needed my morning caffeine fix. I stumbled to the kitchen, Prozac yowling at my heels for her breakfast. I tossed her some Fancy Mackerel Guts and grabbed the instant coffee. For a minute I felt like skipping the hot water and just spooning the stuff into my mouth. But good sense prevailed, and I made my coffee the gourmet way, waiting until the tap water got really hot before adding it to my mug.

After a few sips, I felt my snoozing corpuscles spring to life. I sat down at my computer for the next hour or so, updating my resume, trying not to use the word "Toiletmasters" too much.

When I'd polished my resume as much as it could be polished, I wrapped my hair in a towel and headed for the shower. What I really wanted was to lie back in a nice hot bath, but I couldn't risk any bath-induced frizzies.

After my shower, I padded back to the bedroom, where I stopped dead in my tracks and screamed bloody murder. There was Prozac, sound asleep on my three-thousand-dollar Prada suit! Like a fool I'd laid it out on the bed before stepping into the shower. And now the jacket was covered with cat hairs.

"Prozac, how could you?" I wailed, scooping her up from the bed.

She just yawned in my face, sending a refreshing whiff of mackerel guts my way.

I told myself not to panic. All I needed to do was wrap some packing tape around my hand, and voila! Instant cat hair remover. I hurried to the kitchen only to discover that, voila! I was all out of packing tape. *And* Scotch tape. Damn. I spent the next fifteen minutes picking cat hairs off my suit with the sticky end of Post-its.

Eventually the suit was Prozac-free, and I put it on. Then I threw on some lipstick and blush and flattened my cowlick with industrial strength hair spray. Finally, I filled in the V of my suit jacket with a crystal necklace Lance had picked out from Barneys' jewelry department (another $200 on my credit card).

My toilette complete, I surveyed myself in the full-length mirror on my closet door. I liked what I saw. I was cool. I was chic. I was the new, improved Jaine Austen.

There was only one thing I didn't like. The price tag dangling from the sleeve of my suit jacket. How the heck was I going to keep that thing from popping out? Then I had a brainstorm, or what passed for a brainstorm in my sleep-deprived state. I put a rubber band around my forearm, and anchored the price tag underneath it. It seemed to do the trick. I just had to remember not to move my arm too much.

After a final spritz of hair spray, I grabbed my resume and headed for the door.

"Wish me luck, sweetie," I called out to Prozac, who was in the kitchen napping on a clean dish towel.

She gazed up at me and meowed.

Don't take too long, she seemed to be saying. *I may want a snack.*

When I showed up at Passions, Becky was the only salesperson on the floor.

"Hi, Jaine," she chirped as I walked in the door, her orange hair practically blinding me in the morning sun. "Grace is on the phone with a New York designer, but she'll see you as soon as she's through."

"Fine," I said, trying not to stare at the single gold hoop Becky wore in one ear. Was this some sort of new fashion fad? The Pirates-of-the-Caribbean look?

I guess I must've been staring, because she reached up and felt her naked earlobe.

"Drat," she said. "I dropped my earring again. Darn thing keeps coming off. Oh, here it is." She reached down and picked up a gold hoop from the floor. "One of these days, I've got to get it fixed."

She put her earring back in and looked at me appraisingly. "Wow," she said. "You look great."

"Lance did a makeover on me."

"He did a fantabulous job!"

Fantabulous? I hadn't heard that word since Gidget bought her first surfboard.

"Really. I can't get over how super you look."

Getting a fashion compliment from a girl with Kool Aid hair, purple fingernails, and a vinyl bustier wasn't exactly a rave in *Vogue,* but I was grateful for her kind words.

"Turn around," she said, "and let me get a good look at you."

And it was then that it hit me. I'd hidden the price tag on the jacket, but I'd forgotten all about the tag on the slacks. What if it was dangling down my tush as we spoke?

I smiled weakly and did a half turn.

"Um, do you think I could use the rest room?" I asked.

"Sure."

She pointed out the bathroom, and I scurried to it. It was a small no-frills john with a tiny window opening onto an alley. I checked out my slacks, and sure enough, the tag was showing. Quickly I shoved it under the waistband. I was just about to go back out onto the sales floor when I heard voices coming from the alley.

One of them was the unmistakable voice of Frenchie. And if I had to guess, I'd say the other one was Tyler, the adorable salesman Lance had lusted after. But I didn't have to guess, because by this time, I was standing on the toilet peeking out the window.

What can I say? I'm nosy.

Frenchie was leaning into Tyler, both arms draped around his neck.

"I've missed you, babe," she cooed. "When are you coming back to your Frenchie?"

Tyler looked distinctly uncomfortable.

"Look, Frenchie," he said, removing her arms from his shoulders, "we've been through this a million times. You're a married woman."

"So?"

"So Owen's a nice guy. It's not fair to him."

"Owen doesn't mind. We have an open marriage."

"I think he does mind. I see the way he looks at me and it's not the look of a happy man. Besides, I already told you. I've met somebody new."

"You can't like her more than you like me," she said, running her finger along his upper lip.

"I'm afraid I do," Tyler said, brushing away her hand.

And like that, she turned from pussycat to piranha.

"Nobody dumps Frenchie," she said softly, so softly I had to strain to hear. "You'll be sorry."

It was hot in that small bathroom, but suddenly I felt a chill down my spine. I sure as hell wouldn't want to get on Frenchie's bad side.

Frenchie strode back into the store, the angry click of her high heels echoing in the alley. Tyler just stood there, wiping his lip where her fingers had been. I couldn't tell if what I saw in his eyes was fear or disgust. Probably a little of both.

Then I climbed off the toilet bowl and headed out to meet Grace Lynbrook.

The first thing I noticed about Grace was her hair. It was, to borrow a phrase from Walt Disney, snow white. Which made a startling contrast with the deep blue of her eyes. She had cheekbones as sharp as Ginsu knives, and skin remarkably free of wrinkles. I remembered what Lance said, that she'd been a top model in the seventies. Surely she must've had plastic surgery to look so good. But there were no telltale signs of a surgeon's knife. No slanted eyes, no eyebrows raised in a look of perpetual surprise.

"Jaine," she said, standing up to shake my hand. "So nice to meet you."

She wore white linen overalls with a black tank underneath. Now I can count on the fingers of Venus de Milo's hand the number of women who can wear white overalls and not wind up looking like the Pillsbury

Doughboy. But Grace Lynbrook managed to pull it off. Not only that, her linen overalls—defying the laws of nature—hardly showed a single wrinkle. They wouldn't dare. Not on someone as beautiful as Grace.

I reached out to shake her hand, praying that my price tag wouldn't come zinging out from the rubber band.

"Sit down," she said, gesturing to an overstuffed chintz chair.

Her office, unlike the teak-and-chrome sales floor, was done up country cozy. Her desk was a scrubbed pine table, her chair a white wicker rocker. A back door was open, letting in a cool breeze. It felt like tea time in a Merchant-Ivory movie.

The only jarring note in the room was a battered mannequin propped up against the wall, dressed in faded bell-bottoms and a tie-dyed T-shirt.

"That's Bessie," Grace said, following my gaze. "She's from my very first window display. That's the outfit she was wearing when I opened my shop. I can't seem to let her go, even though she's falling apart. Literally. I've got her arms Scotch-taped to her body.

"Poor Bessie," she said with a laugh. "It's not fun getting old, is it?"

I didn't know about Bessie, but Grace was managing the transition quite nicely.

"Can I get you something to drink?" she offered.

I was dying for some coffee, but didn't want to risk reaching for it and dislodging that damn price tag.

"No, thanks. I'm fine."

She gave me a quick once-over, her electric blue eyes scanning my suit.

"Prada?" she asked.

I nodded.

"Very nice," she said.

Thank heavens for Lance.

"So," she said, smiling a smile that could have lit up the Hollywood Bowl. "Tell me about yourself."

I chatted for a bit about my career as a freelancer, carefully omitting the word Toiletmasters from my spiel.

"Any fashion experience?" she asked.

"Oh, yes," I said, trying to pump some confidence in my voice. "I've done fashion copy."

"Really? Who did you work for?"

"Marida."

"Marida? I've never heard of them."

"It's an Italian company."

"Oh? What do they make?"

"Footwear."

Shame on you if you think I was fibbing. It's true. I did work for a company called Marida. Okay, so it wasn't exactly Ferragamo. Marida was short for Marty and Ida Facciobene, the owners. And the "footwear" they made was extra-wide orthopedic shoes. But technically I wasn't lying, so I don't want to hear any flack about it.

"Sounds interesting," Grace said.

And then she uttered the three words I'd dreaded hearing:

"Got any clips?"

Oh, no. She wanted to see writing samples.

Sighing deeply, I took out a small black portfolio from my attaché case. This was my sample book. In it were several Toiletmasters ads, a Tip Top Dry Cleaners brochure, and a catalogue for Marida footwear, featuring their famous Bunion-Ease Comfort Sandals.

I handed it to Grace, waiting for the ax to fall. But to my surprise, she laughed.

"How marvelously campy," she said, leafing through

my portfolio. "Did you really come up with the slogan *In a Rush to Flush? Call Toiletmasters?* I see it in the Yellow Pages all the time."

"And *Only You Can Prevent Clogged Garbage Disposals,*" I added. "That was mine, too. It won the Golden Plunger award from the Los Angeles Plumbers Association."

She finished thumbing through my book and slapped it closed.

"You're not exactly what I had in mind," she said, "but what the heck. Your copy is pretty damn good. Can you come back next week with some ideas for a magazine campaign? I'll pay you five hundred dollars; five thousand if we use your campaign."

Five thousand dollars? I hadn't seen that many zeros on a check for a long time.

"It sounds great," I gulped.

"Becky can fill you in on the kind of ads we've run in the past. But don't feel limited by what we've already done. Use your imagination."

My imagination was already in overdrive, just trying to picture me, Jaine Austen, a gal who bought her wedding dress from L.L.Bean, writing ads for a trendy boutique like Passions.

Back on the sales floor, Tyler was folding spandex tank tops, studiously avoiding all eye contact with Frenchie, who sat at the register pushing back her cuticles and tapping her Jimmy Choo knockoffs in an angry staccato. You could cut the tension between them with a weed whacker.

I, on the other hand, was remarkably tension-free. Even if I didn't get the job, the $500 Grace Lynbrook was going to pay me for coming up with ideas would at least take my checking account off life support.

I told Becky the good news.

"That's super!" she said, once again channeling Gidget. "Why don't you drop by for dinner tomorrow night, and I'll give you any background information you need."

"You don't have to cook dinner for me," I said. "You've done enough as it is."

"Don't be silly. I adore cooking. I just hope you get the job."

"What job?"

Frenchie was at our side, smiling an icy smile. Why did I get the feeling she could see right through the sleeve of my Prada suit to the price tag inside?

"Jaine might be writing Passions' new ad campaign," Becky said. "She's coming back next week to pitch ideas to Grace."

Frenchie's eyes widened with surprise.

"You're kidding, right? Surely Grace can do better than *her*."

Okay, she didn't really say that. She didn't have time to say that, because at that moment she saw a customer and dropped me like a hot *pomme frite*.

It was the older woman from the other day, the one who dressed like a recycled teenager. Today she was wearing capri's and a mini-sweater, her thin hair pulled back in a pony tail high on her head.

"Mrs. Tucker," Frenchie cooed, "how lovely to see you. I've got a new halter top that just came in. It'll be perfect for you."

And with that, she began plucking clothes off the racks. Mrs. Tucker followed her eagerly, a fashion junkie about to get her fix.

Having deposited Mrs. Tucker in the dressing room with several age-inappropriate outfits, she sailed back to us.

"What a silly old cow," she said, rolling her eyes. "The woman has been under the knife more times than a Benihana steak."

"Frenchie," Becky admonished, "that's not nice."

"You know what I call her?" Frenchie said, obviously not giving a damn about being nice. "I call her Mrs. Nip & Tucker."

"Cut it out, Frenchie," Becky said, a warning note in her voice.

But Frenchie ignored her.

"If I have to lie to her one more time about how good she looks, I'm going to puke."

"Don't worry, Frenchie. You won't have to lie to me any more."

Frenchie whirled around to see Mrs. Tucker, standing outside the dressing room, her eyes blazing.

"You brought me the wrong size," she said, holding up the halter.

Frenchie laughed nervously. "Oh, I wasn't talking about you, Mrs. Tucker."

"Don't you mean Mrs. Nip-and-Tucker?"

For once Frenchie was at a loss for words.

"No, you won't have to lie to me any more, Frenchie. Or to anybody else in this store. Not after I finish talking with Grace. We used to model together, in case you've forgotten. We're friends. *Best* friends."

She stormed off to Grace's office, her surgically taut face even tighter with rage.

"I tried to warn you," Becky said.

"I'm not afraid," Frenchie said airily. "Grace will never fire me. I'm much too valuable to the store."

And with that she went back to the register to contemplate her cuticles.

"What do you think?" I asked Becky when Frenchie was out of earshot. "Will Grace fire her?"

"Gosh," Becky said wistfully. "Wouldn't that be neat?"

Frenchie's fate was of little interest to me as I drove home from Passions. All I could think about was that $5,000 carrot Grace had dangled before my eyes.

I found a parking spot in front of my duplex and was heading up the path to my apartment when I ran into Lance.

"Hey, beautiful," he said, looking me up and down approvingly. "How did the interview go?"

"Great! I'm going back next week to pitch ads for a new campaign."

"Congratulations! Now we have to get you a new outfit. We'll just return the Prada and get something else. Maybe Armani. You can't go wrong with Armani."

"No way, Lance," I said. "I'm not pulling the same scam again. I'm feeling guilty enough as it is."

"But what will you wear?"

"The Prada. I'll wear it one more time, and then I'm going to return it."

"But you can't wear the same outfit twice."

"Why not? I'll just put on a different blouse and change my jewelry."

"I guess it might work," he conceded.

"It'll be fine."

"Are you sure you don't want me to pick up a new blouse for you?"

"I'm sure. I've got a very pretty Ann Taylor blouse I can wear."

"It's not polyester, is it?"

"It's silk. A hundred percent. I swear on a stack of *Women's Wear Dailys*."

After convincing Lance that the world would not

collapse if I showed up in the same outfit twice, we air-kissed each other good-bye, and I let myself into my apartment.

The first thing I did was stow the Prada suit in a garment bag, away from Prozac and her Claws from Hell. The second thing I did was slip into a T-shirt and a pair of elastic-waist pants.

I spent the rest of the afternoon paying bills and getting things done around the apartment.

Okay, so I spent the rest of the afternoon stretched out on the sofa, watching House & Garden Television. But I got to watch a lot of other people getting things done around their apartments. Does that count?

After a Chinese take-out dinner of wonton soup and chicken lo mein (which Prozac was kind enough to let me share), I headed off for a soak in the tub. As I lay there, up to my neck in strawberry-scented bubbles, I could feel my straight Gunterized hair sponging back into tight ringlets. Oh, well. Who cared? I had a whole week before I had to look stylish again.

When my muscles were as limp as my lo mein noodles, I hauled myself out of the tub and slipped into my pink chenille bathrobe, the one with the coffee stains in the shape of the big dipper. Then I toddled to the kitchen, where I treated myself to an Eskimo Pie for dessert.

I was just about to climb into bed when I caught a glimpse of myself in my bedroom mirror. Frizzy hair. Bunny slippers. A fresh ice cream stain on my bathrobe.

In less than twelve hours, I'd gone from Prada to nada.

And frankly, it felt great.

YOU'VE GOT MAIL

To: Jausten
From: DaddyO
Subject: A New Career

Pip-pip and cheerio, old bean!
(That's British for *Hi, Sweetpea!*)

I've been busy as a bee working on my British accent and learning my lines. I figured I might as well memorize the whole part; I'm sure to get it. Your mom has been rehearsing with me. As we theater folks say, she's been "feeding me" my lines.

If I do say so myself, I'm getting better with each reading. In fact, I've been giving it a lot of thought, and I'm seriously considering taking up acting as a career. I could work the dinner theater circuit, and who knows where that might lead? Remember that lady who said, "Where's the beef?" Didn't she break into show biz in her eighties? Heck, I'm a spring chicken compared to her.

All of which leads me to why I'm writing. Don't you have a friend in show business? The gal who writes for a cartoon show? Something about a termite? Maybe she can get me a part on her show. I do a great impersonation of Daffy Duck. It's not an insect, but it's close. Let me know what you think.

To: DaddyO
From: Jausten

Hi, Daddy. Actually, Kandi's show is about a
cockroach, not a termite. And, yes, I do remember
your impersonation of Daffy Duck. It was very funny.
But as far as I know, Kandi's show uses only union
actors. So I'm afraid she won't be able to help you.

Anyhow, good luck at your audition! I'll keep my fingers crossed.

To: Jausten
From: DaddyO
Subject: Not to Worry

That's okay, sweetheart. Playing an insect probably
wouldn't look good on my resume, anyway.

And don't worry about the audition. Like I said, I'm a
shoo-in. My only concern is Mom. She's going to read
with me on stage, and I only hope she doesn't get nervous and flub her lines.

To: Jausten
From: Shoptillyoudrop
Subject: Driving Me Nuts!

Jaine, honey. Your daddy is driving me nuts. I must
have read that silly play with him at least a dozen

times. All he has to read at the audition is two pages, but he insisted on memorizing the whole thing. I tell you if I have to read *Lord Worthington's Ascot* one more time, I'll tear my hair out. (Which reminds me, I bought the most wonderful shampoo on The Shopping Channel. It volumizes while it conditions; two eight-ounce bottles only $19.95, plus shipping and handling.)

But getting back to Daddy. Now he's started talking in a loud hammy voice everywhere we go. He says he's "projecting." He's so darn loud, I'm surprised you haven't heard him in Los Angeles. Yesterday when we were at the supermarket, he said, "Honey, do we need milk?" and seven women answered yes.

It's bad enough I've had to rehearse with him, but now Daddy wants me to read the part of Lady Worthington with him during his audition. He says he's used to reading his lines with me. Honey, I'm a nervous wreck. I can't wait till this silly audition is over!

Love from,
Your frazzled mom

To: Shoptillyoudrop
From: Jausten

Hang in there, Mom. You know how Daddy is. This acting thing is just a Fad du Jour. He'll get bored with it eventually. Just stay calm and don't panic.

To: Jausten
From: Shoptillyoudrop
Subject: The Little People

Oh, Lord. You'll never guess what I just saw! I was walking past the bedroom, and there was Daddy, taking bows in front of the mirror, and thanking "all the little people who made this award possible."

To: Shoptillyoudrop
From: Jausten

Okay, start panicking.

Chapter 6

I drove to Becky's the next night, mulling over the latest news from my parents. Can you believe my father? He hadn't even gotten the part yet, and he was writing his acceptance speech for the Oscars. Honestly, I don't know how Mom puts up with him. She's been doing it for forty years; I guess somewhere along the line she must have built up an immunity.

I parked my car in front of Becky's apartment building in West Hollywood. It was one of those seventies-era singles' buildings that look like they were thrown together with Elmer's Glue and particle board. She buzzed me in, and as I walked down the hallway to her apartment, I could hear stereos blasting through the thin walls.

It was past seven and I was starving. Feeling guilty about that Eskimo Pie I'd had the night before (okay, two Eskimo Pies), I hadn't eaten a thing all day except for a bagel and three Altoids. So when I rang the bell to Becky's apartment, I was ready to eat the curtains.

Becky opened the door, looking adorable in hot pink leggings and an oversized T-shirt. On her feet she wore chartreuse flip flops. Her toenails were painted hot pink to match her leggings, with tiny yellow daisies on each toe.

"Hi, Jaine," she said. "Come on in."

I stepped inside and blinked in amazement. The walls, like her hair, were Sunkist orange, and the furniture—rickety old pieces she'd probably picked up at garage sales—were painted black. I thought I'd died and gone to that great Halloween Party in the Sky.

"Trick or treat!" I said.

Okay, so I didn't really say that. What I said was, "Great apartment."

"I decorated it myself," Becky beamed.

"It makes quite a statement," I said, smiling weakly, thinking that the statement it made was *Redecorate me!*

"Guess what?" Becky said. "I cooked us a steak dinner!"

A steak dinner? My salivary glands went into overdrive.

"You shouldn't have."

And really. She shouldn't have. It turned out that Becky was a vegetarian and the "steak" in question was a hunk of muddy colored tofu, doctored with several "secret ingredients" to make it taste like filet mignon. What it tasted like was congealed motor oil. Not that I've ever tasted congealed motor oil. I'm just guessing.

But I'm getting ahead of myself. Let me start at the beginning of what ultimately turned out to be one of the Top Ten Worst Meals of My Life. Becky sat me down at her black dining table, set with orange place mats.

"I'll be right out with our appetizers," she said, scooting into the kitchen, her flip flops slapping against her heels.

Minutes later, she came back out with two "shrimp" cocktails, actually lumps of tofu rolled in paprika.

"I can't bear the thought of eating a poor defenseless shrimp," she said, popping one of the nuggets into her mouth. "Go on, try it. It's delicious. You'll swear it's shrimp."

I took a bite. It was like swallowing paprika-flavored mucous.

"Yummy," I managed to say, a wooden smile plastered on my face. There was only one way I was going to get through this meal, I decided. With a little help from my friend Mr. Alcohol. I reached for the glass of red wine at my place setting and took a grateful gulp. Only to find out it wasn't wine, but grape juice.

Fasten your seat belt, I told myself, *it's going to be a bumpy night.*

"Eat up," Becky chirped.

I looked at the pink slime balls on my plate. No way was I going to eat them. I gulped down my water and held out the glass.

"Um . . . could I have some more water?"

Becky trotted off to the kitchen. The minute she was gone, I shoved the "shrimp" in my pants pocket. The pants would have to be dry cleaned, but I didn't care. It was worth it.

"My, you sure ate those up in a hurry," Becky said, when she came back with my water. "Want some more?"

Not without a stomach pump, I didn't.

"No, no." I managed another feeble smile. "I've had plenty."

"That's right," she said. "You've got to save room for steak!" She polished off the last of her slime balls. "Isn't this fun? I hardly ever get to cook a meal for anybody. Whenever I invite my friends over, they always want to go to a restaurant."

I just bet they did.

"I'll go get our steaks," she said, with an eager grin.

Just as Becky was coming out of the kitchen with two steaming blobs of brown tofu, the front door opened and a dark-haired pixie in jeans and a tube top came bouncing into the room. Her hair was cut in a 1920s-style pageboy, with a thick fringe of bangs framing her delicate face. But at that moment, I wasn't looking at her hair or her eyes or her delicate face. What grabbed my attention was her hand, which was clutching a McDonald's bag.

"Hi, Nina," Becky said. "Jaine, this is my roommate Nina."

Nina and I exchanged hellos, my eyes still riveted on the golden arches. Then Nina joined us at the table. She opened the McDonald's bag and took out a Quarter Pounder and a double order of fries. God, it smelled good.

"Jaine's going to be writing some ads for the store," Becky said.

"Super," Nina said, flashing me a grin. "I just adore writers."

That's what Becky said yesterday at Passions. Why did I get the feeling that the only thing either one of these girls read on a regular basis were the instructions on a Clairol bottle?

"I don't know how you can eat that yucky meat," Becky said, as Nina squished a blob of ketchup on her hamburger bun.

"It's easy. Watch."

She took a big bite, the burger oozing out at the sides. It was all I could do to keep from grabbing it out of her hand.

"Well, dig in!" Becky said to me.

I looked down at the steaming mound of brown glop on my plate. Next to it was a mound of yellow glop, and another mound of green glop. The yellow glop,

Becky informed me, was squash soufflé, and the green glop was bean sprouts.

Nina looked at our plates and wrinkled her nose in disgust.

"I don't know how you can eat *that* stuff," she said. "I read about this woman who ate too many bean sprouts, and they clogged up her insides so bad, they had to cut her open and take out two feet of her intestines. They found poop in there that was six months old."

Nothing like some sparkling dinner conversation to go with my tofu steak.

Nina shot me a look of pity.

"Want some fries?" she asked.

"No," Becky said, "she doesn't want any fries. Not with all that yummy squash. Right, Jaine?"

"Well, maybe just a few," I said, snagging myself a handful.

I practically inhaled them.

Nina popped the last of her burger in her mouth and licked her fingers. Would this torture never end?

"I'd better get dressed for work," she said.

"Nina's a nurse," Becky explained. "She works the night shift."

I only hoped she didn't regale her patients with tales of clogged intestines and petrified poop.

Nina went to change, and somehow I managed to force down a respectable portion of the meal. There was enough estrogen in all that tofu to keep me going through menopause.

When I was through, Becky scooted off to get dessert, a depressing assortment of sugar-free, fat-free cookies. Accompanied by an herbal tea a most unsettling shade of green.

As I gnawed on a cookie, Becky filled me in on the kinds of ads Passions had run in the past.

"There's not much to tell," Becky said. "Grace always says she wants to do something different, but she always winds up with a straight fashion shot and the Passions logo."

That was it? She could've told me that in two seconds back at the store. But, of course, by this time I knew why Becky had invited me over. She just wanted somebody to cook for. And I was happy to be her culinary victim. Okay, so I wasn't exactly happy. Technically, I suppose you could say I was miserable. But, as I kept reminding myself, Becky was a sweet kid, and without her, I wouldn't have had the interview in the first place.

"Hey," Becky said, when I'd managed to gag down a cardboard cookie, "how would you like to see some of my clothing designs?"

"I'd love it," I said. Anything to put an end to this god-awful meal.

Becky jumped up and minutes later was back from the bedroom with an armful of her designer creations. Now I'm no fashion maven, as Lance would be the first to tell you, but the outfits were a tad strange. Lots of floral prints and black leather. Laura Ashley meets the Marquis de Sade.

"Aren't they awesome?" Nina said, coming out from the bedroom in her nurse's uniform.

"Awesome," I parroted.

Becky's eyes shone with pride.

And who knew? Maybe she really did have talent. Her clothing looked a lot better than some of the stuff that passes for haute couture on the Paris runways.

I did my best to act enthused, and just as I was running out of oohs and aahs, the doorbell rang.

Becky raced to get it.

It was Tyler, looking even cuter than he had at Passions. At the store, he'd worn the tight trendy stuff they stocked. But he'd changed out of his spandex gear into khakis and a button-down shirt, looking very much like the aspiring novelist Becky had said he was. He'd washed out the gel that had kept his sandy brown hair slicked back, and now it flopped boyishly onto his forehead.

He was a decade too young for me, but I still found him adorable. Apparently I wasn't the only one. Because just then Becky threw her arms around him and kissed him on the mouth. He kissed her back with a good deal of enthusiasm.

A little birdie told me this was not a platonic relationship.

"You're Tyler's girlfriend?" I blurted out. "The one he dumped Frenchie for?"

They both nodded.

"We're trying to keep it a secret at the store," Tyler said. "Frenchie would go ballistic if she knew."

"Let her go ballistic," Becky said. "Grace is probably going to fire her, anyway."

"We can only hope," Tyler said.

"Hey, sweetie," Becky said. "Want some soy steak? I've got plenty left over."

"No thanks, Beck," Tyler said quickly. "I already ate."

His eyes shifted nervously, like a deer who'd just narrowly escaped a hunter's bullet.

"Well, I'd better be shoving off," Nina said, grabbing her keys.

"Me, too," I chimed in. I got the feeling Tyler and Becky wanted be alone. Mainly because they couldn't keep their hands off each other's fannies.

"Don't go yet," Becky said halfheartedly.

"No, no. I'll be going. And thanks for everything."

"Did you really like the dinner?"

It wasn't easy, but I managed to say yes.

Nina and I said our good-byes and headed down the corridor to the elevator together.

"Tyler's a great guy," Nina said.

"Yes, he seems awfully sweet."

"An angel. And it's about time."

"What do you mean?"

"Becky has this thing for rotten guys. She always goes for the nogoodniks. It comes from low self-esteem."

"Really?"

"Yeah," Nina said, tossing a piece of bubble gum in her mouth. "I took psychology in nursing school. That's her problem all right," she said, blowing a big pink bubble.

Right on, Dr. Freud.

"But it doesn't matter now," she said. "At last, she's found a winner."

The elevator came and we rode down, Nina blowing bubbles en route. I only hoped she didn't work in neurosurgery.

After saying good-bye to Nina, I retrieved my tofu shrimp from my pants pocket and tossed them in a trash can.

Then I got in the Corolla and drove as fast as I could to the nearest McDonald's.

Chapter 7

The only job in my in box was another resume, this one for a college grad whose career goal was "to do something, like, really fun." I knocked it off quickly, which left me almost a week to work on the Passions campaign.

For those of you interested in how a professional writer works on a major ad campaign, here's my typical schedule:

First I sharpen a bunch of pencils. Then I do the crossword puzzle, just to limber up my brain. Then I grab a snack. Then I scratch Prozac's belly for good luck. Then I grab another snack. Then I check out the news headlines on AOL. Then I sharpen some more pencils. And so forth and so on until it's time for *Oprah,* and *Judge Judy* and dinner.

It's disgraceful, I know. What can I say? I work best under pressure.

And which is why, the night before my pitch to Grace, all I had to show for my labors were some sharpened pencils and a well-scratched cat.

Oh, well. It was only six o'clock. If I worked nonstop for the next five hours, surely I'd come up with something. And then I realized: I was teaching my class that night. Damn. It looked like I was going to have to pull an all-nighter.

Annoyed with myself for having frittered away so much time, I fed Prozac her dinner, wolfed down some ancient Tater Tots I found at the back of my freezer, and headed off to the Shalom Retirement Home.

When I showed up at Shalom, I found a half-eaten package of Twinkies at my place at the head of the table.

"For you, sweetheart," Mr. Goldman said, with a wink.

"Thank you," I said, smiling weakly.

"I hope you don't mind," he said, brushing cupcake crumbs from his vest. "I ate one."

Ah, nothing says *I love you* like used food.

"Okay, class," I said. "Who wants to read first?"

As usual, Mr. Goldman's was the first hand in the air.

I looked around the class, hoping someone else would volunteer. But nobody so much as lifted a pinkie.

"Okay, Mr. Goldman," I sighed. "Go ahead."

He whipped out his notebook with a flourish and began reading.

"My Gallbladder Surgery, by Abe Goldman."

With all the confidence of Lincoln reading the Gettysburg Address, Mr. Goldman proceeded to tell us about his gallbladder surgery, how all the nurses flirted with him, how the surgeon said it was the biggest gall-bladder he'd ever removed in all his years of practice, and how—when he was finally allowed to have visitors—Debbie Reynolds showed up with a big bouquet of roses.

"Oh, please!" Mrs. Pechter said, her huge bosoms heaving with indignation. "Don't start with Debbie Reynolds again."

"Yeah," Mrs. Rubin chimed in. "Enough already!"

"Are you sure you weren't hallucinating?" Mrs. Zahler asked.

"No, I wasn't hallucinating," Mr. Goldman snapped. "Debbie Reynolds visited me in the hospital!"

"Right," said Mrs. Pechter. "Just like Tom Cruise came to see me when I had my corns lanced."

The other ladies chortled gaily. Mr. Goldman glared at them and slammed his notebook shut.

Score one for Mrs. Pechter.

"Okay, who wants to read next?" I asked.

Mr. Goldman's ignominious defeat in the war of words with Mrs. Pechter seemed to have given the other ladies courage. Several hands shot up. And I was thrilled to see that one of the volunteers was Mrs. Stein.

Lillian Stein was a recent arrival both at Shalom and in my class. A plump woman with large sad eyes, she reminded me of a child on her first day in kindergarten. For weeks I'd been hoping she'd read something, but she'd just sat in her chair, silently taking in the chatter around her.

And now, at last, she was raising her hand.

"Mrs. Stein!" I said. "I'm so glad you've got something you want to share with us. Go ahead."

The other ladies murmured their encouragement.

With trembling hands, she unfolded a single piece of lined paper.

"My Husband, Max," she read, in a thin, barely audible voice.

"Speak up!" Mr. Goldman said. "We can't hear you."

"Yes, Mrs. Stein," I said. "A little louder, please."

She began again.

"My husband, Max, and I were married for fifty-two years before he died of a fatal heart attack."

A wave of tsk-tsks rippled through the room.

"We met when I was working in the men's department at Macy's, and Max came in to buy a tie. I could tell he liked me because he wound up buying five ties. And two suits. And a coat."

The ladies chuckled appreciatively.

"He asked me out on a date to go bowling. I didn't much like bowling, but I said yes irregardless."

Mr. Goldman's hand shot up.

"Mistake!" he cried. "There's no such word as 'irregardless'!"

I could see what was happening. Still steamed at having been bested by Mrs. Pechter, Mr. Goldman was now taking out his irritation on poor Mrs. Stein. But he was right, of course. There was no such word as "irregardless."

"Let's save our comments for later, shall we?" I said. "Go on, Mrs. Stein. You're doing beautifully."

Looking somewhat shaken, Mrs. Stein resumed her narrative and told us about her honeymoon, how she and Max drove across country on Route 66, taking in such sights as the Grand Canyon and the Black Hills of North Dakota.

"Another mistake!" Mr. Goldman shouted. "You can't get to the Black Hills from Route 66."

"Oh, for Pete's sake," Mrs. Pechter said. "Put a sock in it, Abe."

"I'm just making a simple correction. After all, I

was a traveling salesman for fifty years. I oughta know where Route 66 goes."

By now, Mrs. Stein was close to tears.

"Mrs. Stein is not writing an atlas, Mr. Goldman," I said. "She's writing a memoir. Let's listen to her, shall we?"

There was no mistaking the anger in my voice.

"Go on, Mrs. Stein," I said, with an encouraging smile.

Reluctantly, Mrs. Stein picked up her paper, which was now damp with sweat, and continued.

My Max was always a good cook, and after we settled in Los Angeles, he opened a restaurant. He called it Max's Delicatessen.

Once again, Mr. Goldman sprung to life.

"You owned Max's Deli?" he asked.

Mrs. Stein nodded.

"On Fairfax Avenue?"

She nodded again.

"I ate there all the time!" Mr. Goldman said.

Mrs. Stein smiled gratefully.

"It wasn't so hot," he said, with a shrug. "The pastrami was too fatty."

Mrs. Stein's lower lip began trembling, and before I knew it she was crying. Here it had taken me more than a month to get her to read, and thanks to Mr. Goldman, I doubted I'd ever see her in class again.

"For crying out loud, Mr. Goldman!" I snapped. "You are the most irritating man I have ever met. In my entire life. You are like nails on a blackboard. Like slow drivers in the fast lane. Like cell phones in a movie. Can't you just shut up and let the poor woman read!"

Yes, I really did say that.

The whole room sat in stunned silence. No one

looked more stunned than Mr. Goldman. Suddenly the color drained from his face.

"My heart!" he said, clutching his chest.

And with that, he keeled over and fell to the floor.

"My God," Mrs. Pechter said. "He's having a heart attack."

"Somebody call 911!" someone kept shouting hysterically. And then I realized I was the one shouting. I grabbed my cell phone and made the call. Minutes later, the paramedics came and loaded Mr. Goldman on to a stretcher.

"Wait," he said, in a feeble voice, as they were about to wheel him out the door. "I've got something to say."

"What is it?" I asked. "What is it?"

"The Black Hills are in South Dakota," he said, a faint smug smile on his face. "Not North Dakota."

Chapter 8

Sleep was out of the question. I was up all night, calling the hospital, begging them to let me know how Mr. Goldman was doing. But because I wasn't a relative, they wouldn't tell me a thing.

To say I had trouble concentrating on the Passions ad campaign would be putting it mildly. I felt about as creative as a washcloth. After a few fitful hours at my keyboard, the best I could come up with was:

Put Some Passion in Your Fashion!

I know it stinks, but you'd stink, too, if you thought you'd just given a helpless albeit irritating old man a heart attack. By the time the sun came up in Beverly Hills, I knew I'd blown whatever chance I had of landing the job.

At 9 A.M. I typed up my ideas, fed Prozac her breakfast, then stumbled into bed for a refreshing half-hour of sleep.

Then I padded off to the shower, where I stood under a spray of icy water, hoping to infuse some life into my body. Too tired to blow-dry the curls out of my hair, I yanked my mop into a careless pony tail.

You'll be glad to know that Prozac went nowhere

near my Prada suit that morning. No, this time, I found her sitting on my last pair of pantyhose, happily clawing them to shreds. Oh, great. Now I'd have to go bare-legged.

After sucking down some tap-water coffee, I got dressed, careful to tuck my price tags out of sight. Then I surveyed myself in the mirror. Let's take inventory, shall we? Bags under my eyes the size of carry-on luggage. Bare legs that needed a shave. Topped off with a headful of Harpo Marx curls. If the folks at Prada had seen me, they would've taken out a restraining order to keep me from wearing their suit.

I tried phoning the hospital one more time, but they still wouldn't give me any information. Then I grabbed my car keys and headed out the door, praying that Mr. Goldman would live to drive me crazy again.

"What happened to you?" Becky said, when I showed up at Passions. "You look like warmed-over dog poop."

Okay, so her actual words were: "Hi, Jaine." But I could tell that's what she was thinking.

"Guess what?" she said. "Frenchie's been in Grace's office for the past hour. With the door shut. Grace was really steamed when she learned about Frenchie making fun of Mrs. Tucker. Isn't it super? It looks like Frenchie's finally getting the ax."

"What a nasty thing to say." We turned to see Maxine, the bookkeeper, clutching a clipboard to her chest. The woman had an uncanny knack for materializing out of nowhere.

"I'm sorry, Maxine, but I meant it. I'll be happy to see Frenchie go."

"How can you say such a thing?" Maxine said, anger

flashing in her tiny raisin eyes. "Frenchie's a wonderful person! One of the nicest people I know."

If Frenchie was her idea of wonderful, she definitely needed to get out more.

"Where's Tyler?" Maxine asked, consulting her clipboard. "He should've been here an hour ago."

"I don't know," Becky said. "I was just wondering the same thing myself."

"Let me know when he gets here. I'm going to have to dock his pay." She started to scuttle back to the cubbyhole where she kept the company books when the door to Grace's office opened.

Frenchie came sailing out, a big grin on her face, not looking the least bit like someone who'd just been fired.

Grace followed her, her face drained of color, like she'd just been socked in the gut with a pair of brass knuckles.

"Listen up, everybody," Frenchie said. "Grace has an announcement to make."

Grace stepped forward and cleared her throat.

"After thirty years in the business," she said, her voice barely audible, "I've decided to retire."

Then she looked over at Frenchie, like an actor in a play who'd forgotten her lines.

"And . . . ?" Frenchie prompted.

"And I'm selling the store to Frenchie."

"What?" Becky gasped.

"You heard her," Frenchie said. "She's selling the store to me."

Becky stood there, wide-eyed with disbelief. Maxine, on the other hand, didn't look the least bit surprised. Was it my imagination, or did I actually see her wink at Frenchie?

"You can come back for your things later, Grace," Frenchie said. "Why don't you go home now?"

Grace nodded mutely, as Frenchie handed her her purse.

I've never seen anyone sleepwalking but I imagine they'd look a lot like Grace did as she stumbled out the front door.

"So you're back," Frenchie said, turning to me. "Here to pitch your ad campaign?"

I, too, nodded mutely. Frenchie seemed to have that effect on people.

"Come in to my office," she said. Accent on *my*.

I followed her as she marched back into Grace's office and opened a large pine armoire. There among assorted loose-leaf binders and fabric samples were some bottles of wine. Frenchie searched until she found the bottle she was looking for.

"Château Neuf du Pape," she said, holding up a bottle of fancy red wine. "Grace was saving this for a special occasion. And I guess this is it."

She opened the bottle and poured some into a wine glass. Then she swirled it in the glass and sniffed. Nodding appreciatively, she took a healthy swig.

"Yummy," she said, not bothering to offer me any.

Not that I wanted a glass of red wine at 10:30 in the morning. But it would have been nice of her to ask. Of course, by this time I already knew that Frenchie wasn't exactly familiar with the concept of nice.

She took another swig of wine and looked around the room, surveying her new domain.

"First thing tomorrow," she said, "I get rid of *that*."

She pointed to the battered mannequin that Grace had saved from her first window display. "You hear that, Bessie?" she giggled. "You're headed for the Dumpster."

Poor Bessie, staring out at us from paint-chipped eyes, almost looked as if she knew what fate was about to befall her.

"You can throw out whatever ideas you've been working on," Frenchie said. "I've already thought of a brilliant campaign."

She plopped down into Grace's white wicker chair.

"The slogan is going to be *Drop Dead, Gorgeous!*"

I suppose it was better than *Put Some Passion in Your Fashion!* But not much.

"And here's the brilliant part," she said. "We're going to have dead people in all the ads. And in the store window, too. Get it? Dead people? As in 'Drop *Dead,* Gorgeous'?"

"I get it," I assured her.

I loathed it, but I got it.

"They won't be real dead people, of course," she babbled on. "They'll be professional models—in coffins, in electric chairs, on operating tables. Beautifully dressed in the latest fashions from Passions. Won't that be fun?"

Right. About as much fun as a hysterectomy.

She slung her feet up on Grace's pine desk, crossing her Jimmy Choo knockoffs and admiring her slender ankles. "All I need from you is some body copy. Stuff about me, and how I've just taken over the store, and my fabulous sense of style."

She wasn't too in love with herself, was she?

"How much was Grace going to pay you?" she asked.

"Five thousand dollars."

She had a hearty chuckle over that.

"I'll pay you three hundred," she said, when she was finished laughing. "And I want the ads on my desk tomorrow morning."

"So soon?"

"It can't take you that long to dash off a few ads," she said. "I'll meet you here at seven A.M."

"Seven in the morning?"

"I'm a morning person. If you don't like it, I'll get someone else."

No way was I going to work for this bitch.

And I was just about to tell her so when the door flew open. Tyler stood there, his boy-next-door features contorted with rage.

"You bitch!" he screamed, taking the words right out of my mouth. "How could you do this to me?"

"I don't know what you're talking about," Frenchie said, with mock innocence.

"Oh yes, you do. You broke into my apartment and trashed my computer. You burned the floppies in my fireplace." By now the veins in his neck were standing out like pieces of twine. "You destroyed my novel. Three years of work down the drain."

"Is that so?" Frenchie smirked.

"I'm filing a police report."

"Go ahead," she said. "You can't prove it was me." She sipped her wine and smiled a sly, taunting smile. "I told you you shouldn't have dumped me."

Then he lost it.

His eyes blazing, he lunged at her, sending her wine glass flying across the room.

"I'll kill you!" he shouted, his hands around her neck.

Good heavens. He was going to strangle her! Not that I blamed him, but it was still awfully scary.

If Frenchie was frightened, she sure didn't show it.

"Go ahead," she challenged him. "You don't have the guts."

And she was right. Slowly Tyler took his hands away from her neck, his shoulders slumped in defeat.

"Now get out of here," she said. "And by the way, you're fired."

He shot her a final look of loathing and headed for the door.

It was then that I started screaming hysterically. No, it wasn't a delayed reaction to seeing Tyler strangling Frenchie. It was because I looked down and saw that my $3,000 Prada suit was splattered with red wine.

"What's wrong with you?" Frenchie asked.

"My suit," I moaned. "It's ruined."

"Not only that, your price tag's showing."

She was right. In all the excitement, the price tag had loosened from its rubber-band mooring and was now dangling around my wrist.

"So you pulled the old 'buy it, wear it, and return it' trick," she said. "I do it all the time myself."

The thought of sharing the same moral zip code with someone like Frenchie made me blush with shame.

"I didn't think the suit was really yours," she added. "You're not exactly the Prada type, are you?"

Now I was the one who wanted to strangle her. Needless to say, I restrained myself.

Just then, there was a knock at the open back door. Two burly men stood in the doorway.

"Delivery from Hollywood Props," one of them said.

Frenchie's face lit up.

"My coffin. Bring it in, guys."

They started wheeling in a gleaming mahogany coffin.

"Bring it out front," Frenchie ordered.

Frenchie and I followed as they wheeled the coffin out onto the sales floor.

"Put it there, in the window," Frenchie said.

"We'll put a corpse in the coffin," she mused aloud, as they hoisted the coffin into the window. "Maybe string one up from a noose. Wow! This'll be hotter than heroin chic!"

Maxine scuttled to her side like Igor at the Frankensteins'.

"Oh, Frenchie," she gushed, her eyes shining with admiration, "you're so creative."

By now, several shoppers had shown up and were watching with interest as the coffin took center stage in the window. No doubt they'd heard the scene in Grace's office. And they were about to witness another one. Because just then, Becky walked up to Frenchie, her jaw tight with anger.

"Tyler told me what you did to his novel, and I think it's just rotten."

"Like I give a shit what you think," was Frenchie's gracious reply.

"Come on, honey," Becky said to Tyler. "Let's get out of here."

She and Tyler started for the door.

"Honey?" Frenchie said. "Wait a minute. Don't tell me you're his new girlfriend?"

"Yes," Becky said, raising her chin defiantly. "I am."

"You left me for this twirp?" Frenchie laughed. "Your loss, Tyler."

"I don't think so, Frenchie," Tyler said. "My loss was ever knowing you."

That seemed to get to her.

"Get out of here, both of you," she hissed. "You're both fired."

Then she turned to me, pointedly ignoring Becky.

"Yes, we'll have corpses in the window. Maybe even a few scattered around the store."

But Becky wasn't about to be ignored.

"Here's an idea, Frenchie," she said. "How about one of those corpses is you?"

A hushed silence filled the room as Becky grabbed Tyler by the elbow and stormed out the door. It was so quiet you could practically hear the sound of Frenchie's blood pressure rising. Flushed with anger, she lashed out at the handiest whipping boy. Namely, me.

"You'd better get started on those ads, Jaine," she snapped, "if you expect to finish on time."

"Are you kidding? You can take your job and shove it up your coffin," were the words I wish I'd been brave enough to utter. But lest you forget, I was now $3,000 in debt, thanks to those wine stains on my Prada suit. I couldn't afford to turn down any job. Not even from an unmitigated bitch like Frenchie. So what I actually said on my way out was:

"See you tomorrow. Seven A.M."

Chapter 9

Happy to make my getaway from Frenchie (or, as I was beginning to think of her, Little Hitler), I headed for the parking lot, where I saw Becky and Tyler standing in the shade of a large jacaranda tree.

Tyler, gaunt and drained of color, looked like a mug shot of himself.

"Are you guys okay?" I asked.

What an idiotic question. How could they possibly be okay? They'd both just lost their jobs, and Tyler had lost his novel as well.

"I'll be fine," Tyler said, "as soon as I've had a martini or three."

"Oh, Tyler," Becky said, frowning. "Do you really think that's a good idea?"

"Yes," he said, "I think it's a spectacular idea."

Frankly, I thought it was a darn good idea myself.

"I don't want to drink on an empty stomach," Becky said. "Let's get something to eat instead. We'll walk over to Pink's. Want to come with us, Jaine?"

The last thing me and my thighs needed was to eat at Pink's. A Los Angeles institution since 1939, Pink's is the Holy Grail for L.A. hot dog aficionados. People come from miles around for their chili cheese dogs, which have approximately nine zillion calories a pop. No, I really had to start watching myself if I ever expected to fit into a single-digit dress size. So Pink's was out of the question. Absolutely, positively out of the question.

"Sure," I said. "Sounds great."

Fifteen minutes later, we were sitting at one of Pink's picnic tables, scarfing down chili cheese dogs and fries, grease dribbling down our chins. Correction. Fifteen minutes later, *I* was scarfing down a chili cheese dog and fries. Becky and Tyler, too upset to eat, barely nibbled at theirs. Why couldn't I be one of those lucky people who lose their appetite when they're upset?

Becky, the vegetarian, had stymied the guys behind the counter by ordering a chili cheese dog without the dog and without the chili. Basically it was a mountain of melted cheese on a bun.

"Tyler," she said, taking a bite the size of a bacon bit, "you've got to call the police and tell them what Frenchie did to your novel."

"Waste of time," he said, shaking his head. "Frenchie's no dummy. I'm sure she didn't leave any fingerprints."

"Then what are you going to do?" I asked.

"Plan A, strangling her, didn't seem to work," he said, with a sigh. "I guess Plan B is to get back to the computer and start all over again. But wait," he laughed bitterly, "I don't have a computer any more, do I?"

"I'd like to kill that bitch," Becky said, with uncharacteristic venom.

Tyler absently stirred one of his fries in a pool of ketchup.

"And what about that weird scene with Grace?" he

said. "I don't believe for a minute Grace turned over the store to Frenchie of her own free will."

"You don't think Grace was ready to retire?" I asked.

"No way," Becky said. "Passions is Grace's life. She'd never step down."

"And how could Frenchie possibly afford to buy the store?" Tyler said. "She doesn't have that kind of money."

"Blackmail," Becky said, waving her veggie dog. A deliciously greasy glob of cheese fell to her plate. Having already inhaled my dog, I eyed it hungrily. I wondered if anybody'd notice if I scooped it up.

"Frenchie's got something on Grace," Becky said. "I'm sure of it. The woman has the ethics of an alley cat."

"Please," Tyler said. "That's an insult to alley cats everywhere."

"You really think she'd stoop to blackmail?" I asked.

"Absolutely," Becky said. "She's already stooped to vandalism. And theft."

"Theft?"

Becky nodded. "You know that Maltese cross she wears?"

"Yes," I said, remembering the chunky gold cross I'd seen nestled in Frenchie's cleavage.

"I'm almost certain she stole it from a customer."

"Really?"

"One day a customer came into the store and said she left her gold Maltese cross in the dressing room. She'd taken it off while she was trying on a sweater. Frenchie and I looked in the dressing rooms, but we didn't find anything. At least, I didn't find anything. Frenchie *said* she didn't find anything. Then two days later, she comes waltzing into the store and guess what she's got around her neck? A gold Maltese cross. She said it was a gift from her husband, but I didn't believe it. Not for a second."

"Why didn't you say something to Grace?" I asked.

"I couldn't. I had no proof. I never saw the customer's cross, so I had no idea if it looked anything like the one Frenchie was wearing. I kept hoping the customer would come back and catch Frenchie wearing the cross, but she never has. Anyhow, I don't doubt for a minute that Frenchie would stoop to blackmail."

"She's got something on Grace, all right," Tyler said. "I just wonder what it is."

"Gosh," Becky said, looking down at her plate. "I've barely touched my lunch. And neither have you, Tyler."

Then she looked over at my plate. Not a crumb in sight.

"Why don't you finish my veggie dog, Jaine?" Becky said, holding out her mountain of cheese.

In a rare moment of restraint, I managed to say no.

I finished her fries instead.

"Just look at my suit! It's ruined!"

I was standing at my bedroom mirror, surveying the damage to my Prada suit. In addition to the wine stains, it now sported a very attractive chili cheese dog grease spot on the elbow of the jacket.

Prozac looked up from where she was napping on my pillow and yawned.

"What am I going to do?" I wailed.

Feed me, of course, was what she seemed to meow in reply. That's her favorite answer to life's difficult questions. That, and *scratch me.*

"Are you never *not* hungry?" I asked.

She shot me a look that undoubtedly meant, *Look who's talking, thunder thighs.*

I started for the kitchen to fix her a snack when the phone rang. It was Lance.

"What do you mean—your suit is ruined?"

Due to our paper-thin walls and the fact that Lance has been blessed with Superman-quality hearing, Lance is aware of a lot of what goes on in my apartment.

"What happened?" he asked.

I told him.

"Oh, Jaine, you always exaggerate. I'm sure it's not that bad. I'll be right over."

Seconds later, he was knocking at my door.

"My God," he said when he saw me. "It's ruined!"

"I told you," I pouted.

"Maybe a dry cleaner can get it out."

I thought briefly of giving it to my old client, Tip Top Cleaners, but I didn't want to give them the business. I was still ticked off at them for deserting me for that ad agency.

"I'll take it to my cleaners," Lance said. "They're the best. They once got out axle grease from my sheets."

"How on earth did you get axle grease on your sheets?"

"It's a long story, involving an old biker boyfriend."

Compared to Lance, I led the life of a convent nun. Heck, compared to most people, I led the life of a convent nun. But my love life wasn't the issue; at the moment all I cared about was the $3,000 I owed the friendly folks at Barneys.

Lance waited in the living room while I changed out of the Prada and into a pair of sweats.

"Are you sure you don't mind taking care of this for me?" I asked, handing him the suit.

"It's the least I can do. Don't forget. I was the one who talked you into borrowing it."

Believe me, I hadn't forgotten.

"Don't look so glum," he said. "I'm sure the cleaners will be able to get out the stains. Well, I'm not totally sure. I'm pretty sure. Well, sort of pretty sure. Maybe."

On that hopeful note, he headed back to his apartment, and I headed for the kitchen to get Prozac her snack.

I'd just tossed a few Chicken-Flavored Tender Tidbits into her bowl when the phone rang. This time it was Mrs. Pechter, calling to give me a medical update on Mr. Goldman.

Thank God, he was still alive. Thank God, Part II, it was only a mild heart attack.

"Try not to worry," Mrs. Pechter said. "He'll be back at Shalom before we know it, reading us his cockamamie stories."

I hung up and breathed a sigh of relief. Mr. Goldman was alive!

I managed to relax for a whole three and a half seconds before the guilt came flooding back. So what if he was alive? He'd had a heart attack, and it was all my fault! If I hadn't yelled at him, he wouldn't be stuck in a hospital bed hooked up to Lord knows how many tubes.

Someday, somehow, I'd make it up to him. But in the meanwhile, I had an ad campaign to write.

Frenchie was right. It didn't take me long to throw together some fawning copy about Frenchie and her fabulous fashion sense. I churned out the ads in a few hours. I would've finished even sooner if it hadn't been for the chili cheese dog raging through my intestinal tract.

After dinner (three Maaloxes and a glass of chardonnay) I collapsed in bed with a hot water bottle on my tummy. Prozac, sensing how uncomfortable I was, plopped down next to me and demanded a belly rub.

Eventually the hot water bottle cooled off, and I tossed it aside. Exhausted from my all-nighter the night before, I fell into a deep sleep. The last thing I remember before drifting off was Prozac curling up in the crook of my neck, her fur soft as silk under my chin.

Maybe my life as a convent nun wasn't so bad after all.

It was dark and drizzling when I drove to Passions the next morning, a perfect match for my gloomy mood. The weather report on the radio said it had been raining all night.

Of course, in L.A., just the mere hint of moisture in the air sends drivers into a tailspin of panic. And so traffic, which should have been smooth sailing at that early hour, was slowed to a crawl. I gritted my teeth in frustration. I only hoped Frenchie was caught in the same sluggish mess.

But when I pulled into the Passions parking lot a little after seven, I saw a silver BMW already in the lot. I assumed it was Frenchie's, because of its vanity license plate: HOTBABE 37. (Amazing, isn't it, that thirty-seven women in the state of California actually think HOTBABE is a neat idea for a license plate?)

Parked under the branches of a jacaranda tree, the BMW was plastered with wet purple blossoms. With all those jacaranda blossoms stuck to the hood, I figured the car must have been parked there for hours. Frenchie wasn't kidding when she said she was a morning person.

I retrieved my ads from the backseat of my Corolla. I hoped Frenchie would like them and wouldn't try to weasel out of paying me. Something told me she was a world-class weasel.

I knocked on the back door, but there was no answer. So I trotted around front, figuring that Frenchie was probably out on the sales floor. But when I got to the street, I was surprised to see that the store was dark. I tried the front door, but there was still no answer.

What the hell was going on? Frenchie had to be in there. After all, I saw her car in the parking lot. Maybe she was in the bathroom. Maybe she was on the phone, calling in a breakfast order to her husband. Or maybe she was just playing some sick Let's-Keep-the-Writer-Waiting game. I wouldn't put it past her.

I stomped around to the back door, cursing her under my breath. This time I knocked with all the gusto of a determined process server. When there was still no response, I tried the door. Much to my relief, it opened. I peered inside, but Frenchie was nowhere in sight.

"Frenchie?" I called out.

No answer. If she was in the bathroom, this had to be the world's longest tinkle.

I headed out to the sales floor. There was something about the front room, shrouded in darkness, that gave me the creeps. All those outfits on display hangers, so spiffy in broad daylight, looked like disembodied ghouls in the dark. I was just about to call it quits and head back to the Corolla when I looked down at the floor and gasped. I hadn't noticed it at first because the room was so dark. But there, lying face down, was a shadowy figure with what looked like a knife in its neck.

At first I thought it was a mannequin. I remembered what Frenchie said about scattering "corpses" around the store as part of her new ad campaign. If this was her idea of high-concept advertising, she was one helluva sicko.

I took a step closer. Strange, I noticed, the mannequin was wearing only one shoe. Then, with a queasy feeling in the pit of my stomach, I realized it wasn't a mannequin, but a human being. It was Frenchie. I recognized her white-blond hair and size-two tush. And now I saw that the blade rammed into her neck wasn't a knife, but the piercing stiletto heel of a shoe.

"Frenchie?" I whispered softly, hoping against hope that this was all part of another sick game, this one called Let's Give the Writer a Heart Attack. But no such luck. She just lay there, stiff as a board. Which is what corpses generally do.

She was dead, all right. Stabbed to death with her own Jimmy Choo knockoff.

Chapter 10

There was no doubt about it. Frenchie was toast. And for the second time in less than forty-eight hours I found myself screaming hysterically and calling 911.

Minutes later, the place was swarming with cops. They plunked me down in Grace's office, where I spent the next hour waiting for the homicide detective on the case to show up. As the cops bustled about their business I heard snippets of their conversation: *"Stabbed in the jugular." "Punctured the carotid artery." "Rigor mortis set in hours ago." "Hey, who stole my blueberry muffin?"*

At last the homicide detective ambled in, a paunchy middle-aged man with sad bloodhound eyes. He looked like he'd seen enough dead bodies to last him a lifetime, although I bet this was the first time he'd ever seen one stabbed to death with a stiletto heel. Then again, this was L.A., land of the strange and home of the weird. Lord knows what the poor man had been forced to witness.

I explained to the detective that no, I wasn't a friend of the deceased, but rather a freelance writer, come to pitch my ads. I assured him that I had no idea who could have possibly done such a terrible thing. Which wasn't totally true. I knew three people right off the bat who would've been glad to see Frenchie vanish from the face of the earth: Tyler, whose novel she'd trashed. Grace, whose store she'd stolen. Even sweet little Becky said she wanted to kill her.

They all hated her guts. But that didn't mean one of them had actually killed her. And I wasn't about to point any fingers. Not after they'd all been so nice to me. I'd let the cops figure it out. That's what they got paid for.

The hound dog detective asked me if I wanted a ride home. I assured him I'd be okay.

"Are you sure?" he asked. "You don't look okay."

"I'll be fine."

As I got up to go, he picked up a Barbie-sized halter top from a rack behind Grace's desk and scratched his head.

"Does anyone really wear this stuff?" he asked.

"Not in my world."

I walked out the back door into the parking lot. By now, the rain had cleared and the sun was shining brightly. I checked my watch. Only 9 A.M. and I'd already discovered a dead body and lost a job. What a ghastly way to start the day.

Sad to say, things weren't about to get much better.

My answering machine was blinking when I walked in the front door. When I pressed the Play button, Mr. Goldman's voice came rasping out of the machine.

Jaine? Are you there? Phooey, I hate these damn machines. Listen, cookie. Mrs. Pechter told me you were worried about me and that you feel responsible for my heart attack. Don't be silly. Just because you yelled at me and I happened to keel over the very next second, that doesn't mean the two are related. Anyhow, the doctor said I can have visitors, so drop by any time. I'd better hang up now. I'm feeling a little weak.

I plopped down on my sofa and sighed. The last thing I wanted to do was visit Mr. Goldman. Not after what I'd just been through. No, a dead body and Mr. Goldman were just too much to handle in one day.

I would've killed for a glass of chardonnay, but it was only 9:30 in the morning. Somehow it didn't feel right pouring myself wine while the *Today* show was still on the air.

It suddenly occurred to me that this was no time to be by myself. I desperately needed some company to help me forget the horror of what I'd just seen. I knocked on Lance's door, but he wasn't home. I tried calling Kandi at work, but she was in a casting session.

I thought of calling my parents, but I didn't want to worry them. I knew they'd have a cow and insist that I come stay with them, or—worse—that they come stay with me. I was desperate, but not that desperate.

I'd just have to distract myself. I'd write a mailer to drum up some new business. After all, I was in dire need of money, what with having to pay for that damn Prada suit. I'd work up an ad, touting my writing skills, and send it off to prospective clients.

I booted up the computer and got down to work. I got as far as . . .

Mailer Ideas

. . . when my mind drifted back to that ghastly scene at Passions. As much as I tried, I couldn't shake the image of Frenchie with that stiletto heel in her jugular.

When forty-five minutes had elapsed and I still hadn't written down a single idea, I gave up on the mailer and tried watching daytime TV. I scooped up Prozac in my arms to keep me company, but the little darling, sensing how stressed I was, wriggled free and wandered to the kitchen to sniff the garbage can.

I don't know how long I sat there, staring blankly at the impossibly beautiful soap stars, not hearing a word they were saying. Finally, I gave up. This was ridiculous. If I had to stay in the apartment one more minute, I'd go nuts. I grabbed my car keys and headed out the door.

As long as I was going to be stressed out, I might as well be stressed out with Mr. Goldman.

Trying to find a patient at Cedars Sinai Hospital is like trying to find a fat woman on network television.

An elderly volunteer at the information desk told me to take the elevator to the fifth floor and follow the blue line on the linoleum until I reached the nurses' station, after which I was to follow a red line and then a green line, and then eventually another blue line. I began the trek feeling a lot like Sir Edmund Hillary must have felt when he decided to take his little hike up Mount Everest.

Several red, blue, and green lines later, I made it to Mr. Goldman's room. The door was half open, and I peeked inside.

Mr. Goldman was lying in his hospital bed, an IV tube attached to his hand, watching Emeril on a TV mounted high on the wall. I knocked on the door, and he looked up.

"Cookie!" he said, waving me over with his remote. "Come in. I was just watching Emeril. He's making fried clams. Feh! He's using too much seasoning.

"Enough with the *Bam!* already!" he shouted at the screen, then clicked off the TV in disgust.

"It's good to see you, cookie," he said, smiling up at me.

"I brought you some flowers."

I held out a bouquet of roses I'd picked up on my way over to the hospital.

"That's nice, darling. Unfortunately, I'm allergic," he said, with a sneeze.

Oh, great. First I'd given him a heart attack, and now I was giving him an allergy attack.

I sprinted out to the nurses' station and gave the roses to a thin-lipped nurse, who shook her head in disapproval.

"You should never bring roses to a hospital," she scolded. "So many people are allergic."

Obviously this was a woman who'd cut class the day they were teaching How to Be Pleasant at nursing school.

I felt like taking them back and giving them to someone who might actually appreciate them, but it wasn't worth it. Instead, I sprinted back to Mr. Goldman's side. In the bright light of day, I could see every line and liver spot on his face. There was something so sad about those liver spots, so vulnerable; just the sight of them made me feel guiltier than ever.

"So," I said, "how are you doing?"

"I'll live," he said, shrugging his narrow shoulders. He seemed so much tinier than he did in class.

"Oh, Mr. Goldman. I feel awful about what happened."

"Don't be silly. Like I already told you, just because you yelled at me and I had a heart attack, that doesn't mean you caused it."

"If there's anything I can do to make it up to you, just name it."

"As a matter of fact," he said, "there is."

"What?" I asked. "What can I do?"

He smiled hesitantly.

"Well, you see, I told Mr. Perez you were my girlfriend."

"Mr. Perez?"

"The guy in the next bed." He pointed to the bed next to him. From the rumpled sheets and dent in the pillow I could see someone had been lying there, but it was empty now.

"He's in the toilet," Mr. Goldman explained.

"Why would you tell him I'm your girlfriend?"

"I know I shouldn't have, but he was bragging about his young girlfriend and what a hot number she was, acting like a real Romeo. And suddenly it just popped out of my mouth. I said I had a young girlfriend, too. You're the only young gal I know so I told him it was you. So would you mind very much pretending to be my fiancée?"

Are you crazy? I felt like shouting. *Of course I mind!*

But then I looked down at those pathetic liver spots. And before I could stop myself, I was saying:

"Sure. I don't mind. Not at all."

At which point we heard a toilet flush in the adjacent bathroom.

"By the way," Mr. Goldman said, "I told him we have nicknames for each other. You're my Honey Bunny, and I'm your Teddy Bear."

Quick. Somebody get me a barf bag.

The bathroom door opened and an old man the size

of a Keebler elf came shuffling out. *This* was the hospital Romeo?

"Hey, Perez," Mr. Goldman said, holding my hand. "Here's my girlfriend I told you about."

"How do you do?" Mr. Perez said, with a wink. "You weren't kidding, Goldman, when you said she was a hot mama."

"She sure is," Mr. Goldman grinned. "Isn't that right, Honey Bunny?"

Where the hell was that barf bag?

"I like my women with a little meat on their hips," Mr. Perez said, looking me up and down appraisingly.

"Personally, I prefer my men ambulatory and not yet on Medicare," was what I felt like saying. But you'll be happy to know that I reined myself in and plastered a phony smile on my face.

We spent the next fifteen minutes in strained chitchat, Mr. Perez filling me in on the details of his hernia surgery. (He had a hernia the size of a grapefruit, in case you're interested.) All the while, Mr. Goldman held my hand in a death grip, refusing to let go, and peppering his conversation with a rash of Honey Bunnies.

Just when I thought my face was going to crack from smiling so much, a tiny woman came hobbling into the room on a cane. She wore her bleached blond hair in a towering beehive and had on enough makeup to cover Tammy Faye Bakker and still have some left over for Ivana Trump. But no amount of makeup could hide the fact that she was somewhere in her eighties.

"Hi, Ramón!" she said, planting a kiss on his cheek. "How's my fella?"

It turns out that this was Mr. Perez's hot "young" girlfriend. At last, Mr. Goldman had met his match in the Vivid Imagination Department.

She may not have been young, but this old dame sure was hot. I watched in amazement as she plunked herself down on Mr. Perez's bed, and they started exchanging kisses. Yikes. Any minute now, they were going to be necking. I had to get out of there before Mr. Goldman got any ideas.

"So nice to meet both of you," I said, "but I've got to be running along."

"So soon?" Mr. Goldman asked.

"Yes, Teddy Bear. I've got a dentist's appointment. Root canal. Can't possibly cancel."

I started for the door.

"Wait a minute," Mr. Goldman said. "Aren't you going to give your Teddy Bear a kiss?"

Gritting my teeth, I walked back to his side. I bent down and pecked him chastely on the cheek.

"That's it?" he asked.

"That's it," I said firmly. "Wouldn't want to get you all excited and give you another heart attack, would we?"

And then I got the hell out of there. As fast as my meaty hips could carry me.

Chapter 11

The minute I came home, I headed straight for the bathtub, tearing off my clothes en route. After all I'd been through, I desperately needed a good long soak. There's nothing like a soothing bath to make a person forget dead bodies and dirty old men.

I'd just filled the tub with my favorite strawberry-scented bath oil and was watching the water begin to bubble when the phone rang.

Like a fool, I answered it. It was Kandi.

"I'll pick you up at seven," she announced.

"For what?"

"Don't tell me you forgot. Tonight we're going speed dating."

"I'm sorry, Kandi, but I can't possibly go."

"Why not?"

"I've had sort of a bad day."

"You're not the only one, kiddo. It's been hell on the set. The actor who plays Fred the Flea got busted on an indecent exposure charge, and we've been casting new fleas all day."

"I think my bad day can top your bad day."

I told her about discovering Frenchie's body.

"Wow," she said. "Death by designer shoe."

"Actually, Lance says they were knockoffs. But the thing is, Kandi, I'm pretty shaken up."

"You poor thing," she said. "But that's all the more reason to get out tonight. You need the distraction."

"I suppose you're right," I conceded. I didn't exactly relish the thought of staying home and thinking about Frenchie all night.

"Okay," I said. "I'll go."

"Good. What're you wearing?"

"At the moment, nothing. But don't worry. I'll choose an appropriate manhunting outfit."

And so—one marathon bath later—I gussied myself up in jeans, an Ann Taylor blazer, and my very best Hanes T-shirt. I topped off my ensemble with a pair of dangly silver earrings my mother had sent me from Home Shopping.

"You don't look too bad," Kandi said, when she picked me up.

"Stop. You're killing me with compliments."

"No, I mean it. It's sort of the Hip Writer look. It works for you."

"I'm so glad you approve."

Ignoring my sarcasm, she put the car in gear and took off for the Starbucks where our speed dating was scheduled to take place. As always, Kandi was dressed impeccably. Tonight she had on designer slacks and a cashmere sweater. I'm sure her knee-highs cost more than my entire outfit.

"Now tell me about that corpse you discovered," she said. "I can't believe you found another dead body."

"I know. I'm still recovering from the one I found last year."

It's true. Last year I found a body in a bathtub

(which you can read all about in *Killer Blonde*, now available in paperback at a bookstore near you).

"Who do you think could have done it?" Kandi asked.

"Just about anyone who ever met her. Frenchie was not a popular person."

"Frankly, Jaine, it's getting a little creepy the way you keep stumbling onto dead people."

"I know. I'm beginning to wonder if maybe I was a mortician in a previous life."

"Just promise me you won't get involved."

"Don't worry. I can't afford to spend time on a murder investigation. I've got to land a writing assignment before my checking account hits the single digits."

Kandi looked over at me, concerned. "You need some money, sweetie? How much?"

That's one of the things I love about Kandi: her generosity. She's always offering to bail me out of my financial scrapes. But as much as I'm tempted, I can never bring myself to say yes. It's a matter of pride, I guess.

"Thanks for offering, hon. But I'll manage."

"Are you sure?" she asked. "I'd be happy to do it."

"I know you would. That's why you're such a special person."

"Oh, sweetie," she said, squeezing my hand. "You know how I feel about you. You're . . . the biggest moron I've ever seen in my entire life!"

"What?"

"I wasn't talking to you, hon." She stuck her head out the window and yelled to the driver in front of her. "If you were driving any slower, you'd be going backwards!"

With the reckless abandon of a stunt car driver, she

pulled out from behind the slowpoke in front of us and wove her Miata in and out of traffic until at last she screeched into the Starbucks parking lot.

When I finally managed to pry my white knuckles from the door handle, I checked out my hair in the passenger mirror. Not too bad. Curly, but not the dreaded Finger-in-the-Electric-Socket look.

"Now, remember," Kandi said, applying a fresh coat of mascara to her already thick eyelashes, "I want to see a smile on your face tonight. Be open and receptive. And sit up straight. No slouching."

"For such a special person, sometimes you can be a real nag."

"That's what best friends are for."

Then she grabbed me by the elbow and marched me in to Starbucks and the wonderful world of speed dating.

Speed dating, for those of you wise enough never to have tried it, is like musical chairs. You sit and talk to a guy for three minutes. At the end of the three minutes, somebody blows a whistle, and the guy gets up and moves on to the next victim—I mean, woman. Except that in musical chairs, there's always a possibility that you won't find a chair and you can stop playing. No such luck with speed dating. Once the game starts, you're stuck there till the bloody end.

For the next hour, I sat in Starbucks, sipping a latte the size of a small rowboat, and answered questions like *How would you describe the inner you?* (Translation: *What do you look like naked?*), *Do you consider yourself spontaneous?* (Translation: *Will you sleep with me on the first date?*), and *What are your favorite hobbies?* (Hoped-for response: *Watching football and fellatio*).

It was like being trapped in a bad episode of *Love Connection*. I can't remember all the guys I met that night. Although, believe me, I'm trying.

There was the pharmacist with a nose hair problem, and the guy who blathered on endlessly about his boat. There was the insurance salesman who, clearly deciding he wasn't interested in me, switched gears and tried to sell me a term life insurance policy. For a while I chatted with the manager of a Krispy Kreme donut shop who gave me a coupon for a free jelly donut. (If it weren't for his bad breath, and the colorful assortment of donut crumbs in his beard, I might have even considered going out with him.)

But the highlight of my night had to be the unemployed actor who spent our entire time together talking to his agent on his cell phone.

At last, the final whistle was blown. Questionnaires were handed out, and we were instructed to put a check mark next to the people we were interested in dating. Sad to say, I couldn't bring myself to make a single check mark.

After an emergency pit stop at the ladies' room (which is what happens when you gulp down a latte the size of a small rowboat), I grabbed Kandi and we headed out to the parking lot.

"So who did you say yes to?" Kandi asked when we got in the car.

"Nobody," I confessed.

I cringed, waiting for the onslaught of recriminations. But Kandi was surprisingly understanding.

"I don't blame you. What a bunch of goofballs. Except for Anton, of course."

"Anton? I don't remember anybody named Anton."

"He wasn't one of the speed daters. He was the

Starbucks guy at the espresso machine. He asked me out."

"You've got a date with a Starbucks guy?"

I couldn't help but be surprised. After all, this was a woman who brought home major bucks writing for a cartoon cockroach. I couldn't see her dating someone who earned his living steaming milk for cappuccinos.

"That's not his real job," Kandi said, her eyes shining with excitement. "Anton is a performance artist. He's only working at Starbucks until he gets discovered."

(Why is it that 98 percent of the people in Los Angeles are waiting to be discovered? Doesn't anybody in this town have a job they actually like?)

"I've always wanted to date a performance artist," she said dreamily. "They're so bold and imaginative. Not afraid to take artistic chances."

By this time, Kandi was mentally ordering the flowers for her wedding. That's the way she is. She meets a guy and right away she's convinced he's Mr. Wonderful. As opposed to yours truly, who understands that behind every Mr. Wonderful there's a Mr. Blunderful waiting to make an appearance.

Kandi spent the rest of the ride home babbling about Anton. Then she dropped me at my place and sped off on a cloud of unrealistic expectations.

Grateful that this horrible day was finally grinding to a halt, I let myself into my apartment, where I had an apple and went straight to bed.

Okay, so I didn't go straight to bed. I got in my car and drove over to the nearest Krispy Kreme. I couldn't let that coupon go to waste, could I?

Chapter 12

When I walked into my apartment I had a funny feeling that something wasn't right. I told myself I was being silly. It was just the stress of the day coming back to haunt me.

I headed to the kitchen to pour myself a much-needed glass of chardonnay. I was just reaching for the wine when I looked up and saw that the kitchen window was open. I broke out in a cold sweat. I never left the kitchen window open. Somebody must've broken in. I raced to the living room and called out for Prozac, but she was nowhere in sight.

With my heart pounding, I headed for the bedroom. She wasn't there, either. I was about to go back to the living room when I glanced in the mirror over my dresser and saw the reflection of someone hiding in the shadows of my closet. Before I could stop myself, I let out a terrified yelp, and a man in a ski mask came lurching out into the room.

Oh, my God. It was Frenchie's killer. I was sure of it. I'd probably seen something incriminating at the scene of the crime, some detail I hadn't yet focused on, something that I might remember later and tell the cops. And the killer, taking no chances, was here to make sure that I kept my mouth shut. Permanently.

I tore out of the apartment down to Olympic Boulevard, my assailant in the ski mask in hot pursuit. By now I was screaming for help, but none of the people in the cars whizzing by stopped to help me. What was wrong with them? Couldn't they see I was in trouble?

I looked up and saw that I was approaching Crazy Eel, a popular sushi restaurant. They had a valet parking lot in back. The valets would surely help me. I dashed down the alley to the parking lot. But when I got there, it was empty. No valets. No cars. The only thing there, I saw to my horror, was a coffin. Parked in a handicapped space.

I whirled around and my assailant in the ski mask was right behind me. In his hand, he held a Jimmy Choo shoe, its long lethal heel glinting in the moonlight like a dagger. I tried to run, but I was frozen with fear. My assailant laughed, a shrill, piercing laugh, then reached up and pulled off his ski mask.

I gasped at what I saw. The face under the mask wasn't a face at all—but a jelly donut! With raspberry jelly oozing out of it. Then the creature started laughing again, that awful, piercing laugh, which now sounded just like a phone ringing.

In fact, it *was* a phone ringing. My phone. Groggily I woke up and realized that I was safe at home in bed, Prozac nestled on my chest. Thank heavens, it was only a dream, a reaction no doubt to Frenchie's murder and the two Krispy Kreme jelly donuts I'd scarfed down at midnight.

(Okay, three Krispy Kreme jelly donuts.)

I reached over and answered the phone.

"Have you heard the news?" Lance's voice came on

the line. "That bitchy salesgirl at Passions got killed last night."

"Yeah, I know. I was the one who discovered the body."

"My God! I want all the details!—Wait, hold on. There's my other line."

While I waited for Lance to take his other call, I glanced down at the floor and flinched at the sight of an empty Krispy Kreme donut box inches from my bed. Just a few crumbs remained. And I'm ashamed to say I ate them.

"That was Becky," Lance said, coming back on the line. "The cops think she killed Frenchie."

"That's crazy," I said, thinking that maybe it wasn't so crazy after all. Hadn't Becky said just yesterday that she wanted to kill her?

"I told her about the murders you've solved," Lance said, "and she wants you to help her out."

Just then I heard a call-waiting click on my line. "Lance, I've got another call."

"Better take it. It's probably Becky."

And it was.

"Oh, Jaine," she wailed. "The police think I killed Frenchie. They came to question me yesterday, and I just know they thought I did it. Anyhow, I was hoping you could find the killer. Lance told me you've solved a few murders."

"That's true," I said, with no small amount of pride.

"Good. Because I can't afford a real detective. They're expensive."

She couldn't afford a *real* detective? What did that make me? Chopped liver?

"But I could pay you something," she said, sensing my hesitation. "Say, two hundred dollars a week?"

Barely minimum wage, but it was better than the absolute zero I was currently earning.

"I'll be right over."

I threw on some clothes, fed Prozac her morning mackerel guts, and headed out the door, almost tripping over the *L.A. Times* on my front step.

Frenchie's murder was headline news: *Woman Slain in La Brea Boutique.* According to the story, the cops hadn't made an arrest, but had a suspect they were investigating. I checked to see if my name was mentioned in the article, but all it said was that an unidentified woman had discovered the body. Good. The last thing I needed was for my parents to get wind of my involvement in the murder.

I started down the path to my Corolla when Lance came bounding out of his apartment.

"So, did you take the case?" he asked.

"Yes. In fact I'm going over to Becky's right now."

"Wait! Before you leave, you've got to tell me all about discovering the body. Don't leave out a single gruesome detail! Is it true what I read in the paper, that she was killed with a shoe?"

I nodded. "One of her Jimmy Choo knockoffs."

"Wow," he said, whistling softly. "Talk about your shoes to die for."

I filled him in on the gruesome details of my discovery, then got in my Corolla and headed over to Becky's.

I was tempted to stop off for an Egg McMuffin en route. But no way was I going to do it. Not after last night's jelly donut fiasco. Instead, I had a hearty breakfast of three Wint-O-Green LifeSavers I found at the bottom of my purse.

So it was with minty-fresh breath that, fifteen min-

utes later, I rang Becky's doorbell. Becky answered the
door in shorts and a tank top, those absurd daisies still
painted on her toenails. Her eyes were red-rimmed
from crying, and her hair was flat on one side of her
head from where she'd slept on it.

"Oh, Jaine," she said. "I'm so glad you came."

I followed her into the living room, where she sunk
down into the sofa. I sat across from her on one of her
black Halloween chairs.

At which point her roommate, Nina, came bustling
out of the kitchen in a sweatsuit, carrying a tray. Even
the baggy sweats couldn't hide her perfect little figure.

"Here, Beck," she said. "I brought you some
chamomile tea, and a gluten-free muffin." She looked
at the muffin and wrinkled her nose. "Ugh. These
things are like cement with raisins."

Becky took the tea and smiled gratefully. "Thanks,
Nina."

"I bought some cheese Danishes, too. Sure you
don't want one?"

Becky shook her head no.

"How about you, Jaine?" Nina held out a plate of
plump cheese Danishes.

No way was I going to eat a Danish. Not with those
jelly donuts already clinging to my thighs. For once, I
was going to be strong and say no. Capital N. Capital
O.

"Sure," I said, grabbing one.

What can I say? I can't take me anywhere.

Nina sat on the sofa next to Becky.

"So, Jaine," she said. "I heard you found the body.
How awful."

"It sure was."

"Stabbed in the neck. What a terrible way to die,"
she said. "I once heard about a guy who was fatally

stabbed by a shish kabob skewer. It was at an all-you-can-eat Iranian buffet, and the poor guy tripped on his way back to his table. Impaled himself on his own shish kabob."

My God. First the story about the petrified poop. And now this. The woman was a walking encyclopedia of medical horror stories.

"Nina, please," Becky said, shuddering.

"Sorry, hon. I'm such an idiot. I didn't mean to upset you." She put her arm around Becky and gave her a squeeze.

"Poor kid," she said, turning to me. "She's been crying all morning."

As if to prove it, Becky's eyes welled with a fresh batch of tears.

"It's all so crazy," Nina said. "Becky didn't kill Frenchie. She couldn't have. Becky wouldn't hurt a fly. Really, she won't even kill a spider. She picks them up with a paper towel and sets them free out front on the sidewalk."

"What makes you think the cops suspect you?" I asked.

Becky blinked back her tears.

"For one thing, Maxine told them what I said at the store yesterday, about decorating the store with Frenchie's corpse."

"But you weren't the only one who said something nasty to Frenchie yesterday. Everybody heard Tyler threatening to strangle her. How come the cops don't suspect him?"

"Because they didn't find Tyler's earring at the scene of the crime."

"What do you mean?"

"They found my gold hoop earring clutched in Frenchie's hand."

I remembered Becky's big gold hoop, and how it had fallen off the day I came to the store for my interview.

"I tried to explain to the police that it's always falling off, but I could tell they didn't believe me."

"She obviously dropped it in the store," Nina said, "and the murderer found it and put it in Frenchie's hand to make it look like Becky did it."

"I realized it was missing last night," Becky said.

"We looked all around the apartment for it," Nina said, "but we couldn't find it."

"So then I knew it must be back at the store. I figured I'd wait and pick it up today. But now I don't know if I'll ever get it back. The cops are keeping it as evi—"

But she never got to finish the "dence" in evidence, because just then she broke out into a fresh batch of tears.

"Honey, please don't cry." Nina put her arm around her and patted her back, trying to calm her down. Finally, Becky stifled a sob and looked at me with pleading eyes. "So will you help me, Jaine?"

"Of course I'll help you." My earlier doubts about Becky had disappeared. I agreed with Nina. I simply couldn't believe this little pixie was a killer.

"Oh, Jaine. Thank you," she said, throwing her arms around me. She smelled of chamomile tea and Johnson's Baby Shampoo.

"I'll pay you two hundred dollars a week," she said when she finally managed to pry herself away. "Just like I promised."

"I can't let you pay me. You don't even have a job."

Wait a minute. Why couldn't I let her pay me? I didn't have a job, either.

"Oh, but Grace called earlier. She hired me back again. Tyler, too."

"That's wonderful."

"So I can definitely afford to pay you. I don't actually have the cash, but Nina said she saw a Web site where I can borrow money for only forty percent interest."

"Forty percent? I can't let you do that."

Why on earth not? I needed the money just as much as she did. More, probably.

"Why don't we see how things work out?" I said. "And you can pay me later."

I'd obviously suffered a minor stroke and lost my powers of rational thinking.

"Oh, Jaine. You're an angel."

An idiot was more like it.

"What I need from you," I said, "are some addresses and phone numbers. For Grace, Maxine, and Tyler. I'm going to have to question all of them."

Becky's eyes widened with alarm. "Oh, you can't possibly suspect Tyler. He couldn't have done it."

"Still," I said, "I'll need to talk to him."

"I've got a staff list somewhere," Becky said. She went over to a telephone table near the front door and started looking through some papers in one of the drawers.

"Here it is." She came back and handed me the address list.

"By the way," she said, "Grace told me there's going to be a memorial service for Frenchie tomorrow. At St. Joan of Arc in Westwood."

"Are you going?" I asked.

She shook her head no.

"I keep telling her she should put in an appearance," Nina said. "If she stays away, the cops will think she didn't like Frenchie."

"They already know I hated her. I told them myself."

"Did you have to be so darn honest?" Nina asked.

"You're right. I was a fool. I practically signed a confession." She wrung her hands in despair. "They're going to arrest me. I just know they are."

And, as if to prove her right, at that moment the doorbell rang. Two cute young cops stood at the door. If they hadn't been in uniform, you'd think they were there to pick up the girls for a double date. But they were in uniform, and this was not a social call. The taller of the two cops, obviously the team spokesman, stepped forward.

"Ms. Kopek?" he asked.

Becky nodded. "That's me."

"I'm afraid we're going to have to take you downtown for questioning."

Surprisingly, Becky didn't cry.

"I'll get my purse," she said, nodding stiffly, then started down the hallway to the bedroom.

"Don't forget a sweater," Nina called out after her. "And put on some long pants. It's chilly outside." Then she turned to me, her brow furrowed with concern. "I hope she doesn't catch the flu. Seven out of a hundred flu cases can lead to fatal complications."

Another fun fact from Nurse Nina.

Minutes later, Becky came back out, in jeans and an oversized sweatshirt.

"Why don't I come with you?" Nina said.

"Sorry," the spokesman cop said. "Just Ms. Kopek."

Reluctantly Nina let her go.

"I was just about to leave," I said. "Do you mind if I ride down in the elevator with you?"

"Not at all," he said, his face as impassive as a piece of toast.

So I rode down the elevator with Becky and the cops. When we got outside I hugged her good-bye.

"Don't worry. You'll be back in no time."

"Yeah, right," she said, her voice tiny with fear.

The cops led her away, her flip flops clacking mournfully on the sidewalk. She slid in to the backseat of the squad car, then turned around and waved at me through the rear window, like a frightened kid leaving home for the first time.

I stood there, watching the car disappear into traffic, hoping the cops would go easy on a girl with daisies on her toes.

YOU'VE GOT MAIL

To: Jausten
From: DaddyO
Subject: No-Talent Hack!

Alistair St. Germaine is a no-talent hack who wouldn't know a good performance if it bit him on the fanny.

To: Jausten
From: Shoptillyoudrop
Subject: The Strangest Thing

Honey, I'm afraid I've got bad news. Daddy didn't get the part. Mr. St. Germaine cast himself in the lead as Lord Worthington. He gave Daddy the part of the butler. Poor Daddy's got only one line: "Very good, sir." Although he does get to say it six different times throughout the play. Needless to say, he's furious.

But guess what? Remember how nervous I was about getting up on stage and feeding Daddy his lines? Well, the strangest thing happened. Once I got up there, I wasn't scared at all. Before I knew it, I was having fun. Anyhow, you'll never believe this (I still can't!), but Mr. St. Germaine was so impressed with the way I read the part of Lady Worthington, he cast me as his leading lady! At first I turned it down. After all, it was Daddy who wanted to be in the play, not me. But Mr. St. Germaine was so persuasive, I just couldn't say no. He said the play wouldn't be the same without me. So your little ole mom is going to play the part of Lady

Cynthia Worthington in the world premiere of *Lord Worthington's Ascot*. Isn't that exciting?

Of course, Daddy is furious with me, and I probably should have turned down the part to keep peace in the house, but like I said, I just couldn't say no to Mr. St. Germaine. Who, by the way, insists that I call him Alistair.

More later—
Mom

To: DaddyO
From: Jausten

Hi, Daddy. Mom told me what happened at the audition. I'm sorry you didn't get the lead. But I'm sure you'll be terrific as the butler.

To: Jausten
From: DaddyO
Subject: The Germ

The only reason I agreed to play the butler in that stupid play is because I want to keep an eye on Mr. No-Talent Alistair St. Germaine. Or, as I call him, The Germ. Frankly, I think The Germ has the hots for your mom. Why else would he cast her as the female lead? Let's face it; your mom is a wonderful woman, but she's no Meryl Streep.

And by the way, I checked out The Germ on Google. It turns out his "Off Broadway" plays were off

Broadway, all right. All the way off Broadway, across the river in Hoboken, New Jersey. What a scam artist.

To: DaddyO
From: Jausten

Don't be silly, Daddy. I'm sure Mr. St. Germaine doesn't have "the hots" for Mom.

To: Jausten
From: Shoptillyoudrop
Subject: You'll Never Guess What Happened!

Oh, honey! You'll never guess what just happened. The doorbell rang, and it was the florist. With a dozen roses from Mr. St. Germaine! The card said, "Congratulations, to my new star." Isn't that just the sweetest thing?

Chapter 13

The sun shone brightly on the day of Frenchie's memorial service. Birds were chirping, flowers were blooming, and fluffy white clouds scudded across a deep blue sky. Clearly Mother Nature didn't give a flying fig that Frenchie's corpse was cooling in the L.A. County Morgue.

I got in my Corolla and headed for St. Joan of Arc church, pondering the latest bombshell from my parents.

So Mom had landed the female lead in *Lord Worthington's Ascot*. Somehow I had trouble picturing her as a British aristocrat. I mean, this is a woman whose idea of a formal event is the opening of a new Safeway.

I wondered if Daddy was right. Could the director possibly have a crush on her? After all, Mom was a very attractive woman. But then, Daddy was a confirmed paranoid. So it was hard to tell. One thing I knew for sure. Daddy would be hell to live with now that he'd been passed over for the male lead. I was just glad I was three thousand miles out of their orbit.

The first thing I saw when I drove up to the church

was a marble statue of Joan of Arc glittering in the noonday sun. I looked at the noble young girl and couldn't help comparing her to Frenchie, who had about as much nobility as a swamp rat.

I parked my car in the parking lot and hurried inside. Only a handful of people were scattered in the large sanctuary.

I slid into a pew and scanned the mourners. I spotted Grace and Maxine, sitting on opposite ends of a pew. Maxine kept looking over at Grace, as if to catch her attention, but Grace sat ramrod stiff, staring straight ahead. A few of Frenchie's fashionista friends sat together whispering in another pew. The only man at the service was a paunchy middle-aged guy in the front row, sobbing into a Kleenex.

The priest, a stocky man who looked like he could have been a football quarterback, was giving a eulogy for Frenchie. I could tell he didn't know her very well because he was talking about what a swell person she was.

"Although Giselle has left us, she will always be with us in spirit."

Not exactly a comforting thought. Did we really need Frenchie's spirit hovering over the planet? Couldn't she just go and aggravate people in the afterlife?

"And now," the priest said, "Giselle's husband, Owen, would like to say a few words. Mr. Ambrose?"

The paunchy guy in the front row got up and headed for the microphone. I blinked in amazement. This was Frenchie's *husband*? I'd just assumed he was her father. He had the dissipated look of a man who'd spent far too much time alone at the end of a bar nursing a bottle of Jack Daniels. Tall and barrel-chested, his thick black hair was riddled with gray. Maybe at one time he'd been a studly guy, but now he looked like an aging Fred Flintstone.

He hadn't gotten more than three sentences into his eulogy when he started sobbing. He tried to calm himself, but he couldn't talk without breaking down. Finally, the priest had to lead him back down to his seat.

"Who else would like to say a few words about the dearly departed?" the priest asked.

No one wanted to say a few words, so the service broke up. From start to finish, it took all of about six minutes.

The priest handed out directions to Frenchie's apartment, where her husband was hosting a "memorial buffet," and the mourners got up to go. As we headed up the aisle, I heard snippets of conversation from Frenchie's fashionista buddies.

"I hear they're shipping the body back to her parents in New Jersey. After the autopsy, of course."

"Want to go to the memorial buffet?"

"Nah, let's have lunch at the beach."

"Oh, yes. That sounds so much nicer."

I hoped Frenchie's spirit wasn't hanging around to hear how breathtakingly fast her friends had gotten over her death.

And then I heard a snippet of conversation that caught my attention.

"Grace, can you ever forgive me?"

It was Maxine. She and Grace were standing on the steps of the church. I stopped and pretended to be reading the directions to Frenchie's apartment while I listened in on their conversation.

"I can't believe I behaved so horribly," Maxine said. Her frizzy brown hair was wilder than ever, and her tiny face was pinched with unhappiness.

What horrible thing, I wondered, had Maxine done?

"I don't suppose you want me working at the store any more," she said, staring down at her support pumps.

"I don't know, Maxine. I'll have to think about it," Grace said.

Unlike Maxine, Grace looked amazingly chipper in a black Prada suit. I knew it was Prada because I'd seen it at Barneys. With her perfectly coiffed white hair and wraparound sunglasses, she looked good enough to hit the runway in Milan.

"I've got to go now," Grace said, checking her watch. "I've got a shipment coming in from New York."

With Frenchie gone, it looked like Grace was back in the saddle at Passions. Then she turned on her heel and walked to her car, a silver Jaguar sedan.

"I'm really sorry," Maxine called after her, in a soft, sad voice.

But I wasn't paying attention to Maxine any more. Or Grace, either.

No, my eyes were riveted on the roof of Grace's Jaguar. Which I now saw was plastered with jacaranda blossoms. I remembered the jacaranda tree in Passions' parking lot, and how the blossoms were sticking to Frenchie's car in the rain. And here they were, stuck to Grace's car. It hadn't rained at all since the night of Frenchie's murder. If these were fresh blossoms, they would've blown away in the wind. But they were stuck on, plastered there by the rain.

And then I wondered: Was it possible that Grace had driven to Passions the night of the murder? Was she the one who stabbed Frenchie with a fake Jimmy Choo and sent her to that Great Boutique in the Sky? Had

Grace been prepared to try anything—including murder—to get her store back?

Frenchie's apartment building was a nondescript concrete box called Malibu Villas. Its name was clearly a figment of the owner's imagination, since it was nowhere near Malibu, and nothing remotely like a villa.

I rode up in a creaky elevator with a pair of twenty-something bimbettes in T-shirts so tight they were practically tourniquets. The place was undoubtedly populated by transient young singles. Frenchie's middle-aged husband must have stood out like a sore thumb.

Owen Ambrose answered the door to his apartment, holding a beer stein filled with what looked like scotch. His florid face was glistening with sweat.

"I'm so sorry for your loss," I murmured.

"Who're you?" he muttered, gazing at me with glassy eyes.

"I'm Jaine Austen. A business associate of Frenchie's."

"Come on in," he said, almost blowing me away with the booze on his breath.

I stepped inside and was surprised to see that the living room was filled to capacity with pricey oversized furniture, the kind of stuff you see in sprawling estates, not a crackerjack apartment with an unobstructed view of the Golden Arches.

"Help yourself to the buffet," Owen said, pointing to a card table draped with a black crepe paper tablecloth.

Frenchie's memorial buffet consisted of pretzels, Cheezits, and a mammoth jug of Costco scotch. It's a good thing he hadn't spent a lot of bucks on the spread, because—aside from me—nobody had shown up.

I grabbed a handful of pretzels and took a seat on a large overstuffed sofa across from a fake fireplace whose electric logs glowed like burners on a hot plate.

"Who'd you say you were again?" Owen asked, squinting at me.

"A business associate of Frenchie's."

He scratched his head, sending a small shower of dandruff to his shoulders.

"I can't understand why more people didn't show up at the church. You'd think they would have wanted to come."

"Only to make sure she was really dead."

Of course, I didn't really say that. I just tsk-tsked sympathetically and stared into the phony fire.

"Aw, who am I kidding," he said, draining the scotch from his beer stein. "I'm not really surprised. Most people didn't like Frenchie. She could be a real bitch. But God, how I loved her."

Clearly the Costco scotch had loosened his tongue.

"I left my wife and kids for her. Just packed up and moved out. After eighteen years of marriage. Arlene didn't deserve to be treated that way. No, she didn't. But what can I say? I was crazy in love."

He hauled himself up from his armchair and weaved his way to the buffet table. I watched, fascinated, as he poured himself another steinful of scotch.

"I knew Frenchie was only interested in me for my money."

Money? I wondered. *What money?*

"I was rich when she met me," he said, as if in answer to my question. "I'd made a fortune in a dot-com startup company. When Frenchie and I were first married, we lived like kings. A five-bedroom house in Beverly Hills. Beach place in Malibu. All this furniture," he said, gesturing around the room, "came from the beach house."

"It's very nice," I said, trying to keep up my end of the conversation.

"But we all know what happened to the dot-com bubble," Owen said, plopping down into his armchair. "Poof!"

He took a frighteningly large gulp of scotch, to get him through that awful memory.

"Once I lost my money, it was all over. Frenchie had no use for me. She cheated on me right and left and didn't bother to hide it. I should've hated her, but I didn't. I couldn't stop loving her. It was like she had me under a spell or something. Like that movie with Marlene Dietrich, where she sings 'Falling in Love Again'."

"The Blue Angel."

"Yeah, like *The Blue Angel*," he said, taking another mammoth gulp of scotch. I could practically see his liver corroding before my eyes.

"Let me get you something to eat," I said.

"Nah, nah," he said, waving me away. "Not hungry. I could do with some scotch, though. Get me some more, will ya, hon?"

He held out his stein, like an alcoholic Oliver Twist.

"Really," I said. "Let me fix you something to eat."

Before he could stop me, I made my way into his tiny kitchen. I rummaged around the mostly empty cupboards until I found a can of tuna. Somehow I managed to toss together a tuna salad sandwich on a stale bagel.

"Here," I said, handing it to him. "You've got to eat something."

Reluctantly he took a bite.

"You know, for something you whipped together on the spur of the moment, this is really pretty bad."

Look who was talking. The Cheezit King.

"Eat it anyway," I ordered. "Or I'll make you another."

I waited till he'd finished eating, then got down to business.

"I don't know if you're aware of it, but the police think Becky Kopek killed your wife."

"Sweet little Becky?" He looked genuinely surprised. "That's impossible."

"Do you have any idea who might have done it?"

"No, not really. Lots of people disliked Frenchie. But I didn't think anybody hated her enough to kill her. Arlene probably would have wanted to kill her at one time. But she's remarried now. To a gynecologist. She says my leaving her was the best thing that ever happened to her. So it couldn't be Arlene. I figure whoever called Frenchie that night must've done it."

"Somebody called her?"

"Yeah, she got a phone call from Passions' alarm company. They said someone had broken into the store. So she drove over. But it turns out the alarm company never called her. Whoever made the call was probably luring her down there so they could kill her."

"Did she say whether it was a man or a woman on the phone?"

He shook his head. "Nah. She just grabbed her keys and ran. And that was the last I ever saw of her."

His eyes filled with tears, and the next thing I knew he was sobbing onto his bagel crusts.

Somehow I managed to get him to lie down on the sofa. Then I wrapped some ice in a towel and put it on his forehead.

By the time I'd grabbed a handful of Cheezits and made my way to the front door, he was snoring like a buzzsaw.

I sat in my Corolla, munching my Cheezits (and the Quarter Pounder I'd bought to go with them), and puzzling over that phony phone call from the alarm company. If someone wanted to lure Frenchie to the store to kill her, why didn't they bring a murder weapon? How could they know in advance that she was going to be wearing lethal heels? Maybe they lured her to the store intending only to confront her, but then things got out of hand, and the next thing they knew they were going for her jugular.

Then again, maybe Owen was lying. Maybe there was no call. Maybe Frenchie went to the store to get some work done, and Owen followed her. His grief seemed genuine, but who knew? Maybe all those affairs of hers finally got to him. After years of being cuckolded, had he assuaged his bruised ego with a deadly fashion accessory?

It was only speculation, of course, but it made sense to me.

I popped the last pickle slice from my burger into my mouth, then put the car in gear and headed off to pay a call on my next suspect, Maxine the bookkeeper.

Chapter 14

Maxine's apartment was out in the valley, on a busy street in Sherman Oaks. The sign out front read *Luxury Apartments*. I gazed up at the beige stucco building with the rusted hibachis on the balconies. If these were luxury apartments, I was a size 2. First Malibu Villas, and now this. What was it with these apartment building owners? Hadn't they ever heard about the concept of truth in advertising?

I parked out front and headed up to *Luxurious Arms*, as I was now calling it. The front path was littered with discarded Thai take-out menus. I found Maxine's name and apartment number on the directory. Luckily someone had left the door open, so I didn't have to buzz Maxine and ask her to let me in. Something told me she might not have said yes.

The lobby was a small square room with gold-flecked mirrored walls. I pressed the button for the elevator. As I waited for it to show up, I thought of Maxine's tearful apology to Grace on the steps of the church. She'd begged Grace to forgive her for behaving "so horribly." What the heck was that all about?

At last, the elevator doors opened, and I got on. I pressed the button for the third floor, and the doors slowly creaked shut. After another eternity, it started moving, squealing and moaning every inch of the way. The elevator had to have been one of Mr. Otis's first models. I was certain that any second now, the cable would snap.

I cursed myself for eating that Quarter Pounder. Just my luck it would be that final quarter of a pound that broke the cord. I could see the headlines now: *Woman in Elastic-Waist Pants Steps on Elevator, Cable Snaps*. I sighed with relief when the elevator finally opened its doors onto the third floor.

I made my way down the corridor to Maxine's apartment and rang the bell. I heard footsteps approaching; then a shadow flitted across the peephole.

Maxine opened the door, in a faded terry bathrobe.

"Jaine," she said, "what are you doing here?"

I couldn't think of a convincing lie to explain my presence outside her door, so I went with the truth.

"Actually, I'm investigating Frenchie's murder."

She blinked, puzzled. "I don't understand. I thought you were a writer."

"I am, but I also do a little private investigating on the side. Do you mind if I come in?"

I guess she minded, because she just stood there, blocking my path.

"I'm sorry," she said. "I already told the police everything I know."

So much for going with the truth.

Just as she was about to shut the door in my face, I felt something furry around my ankles. I looked down and saw an old gray cat. Quickly, I scooped it up in my arms.

"What a darling kitty," I cooed. I guess the cat must

have smelled the Quarter Pounder on my breath, because it started nuzzling my cheek.

"That's Sparkles," Maxine said, smiling indulgently at her cat. "She really likes you."

"The feeling is mutual," I said, scratching Sparkles behind her ears. "She's adorable."

Yes, I was sucking up to Maxine, but I wasn't lying. I think all cats are adorable. And Sparkles was no exception.

"Would you believe she's eighteen years old?"

Actually, I did believe it, but I pretended to be surprised.

"No! Really?"

Maxine nodded sadly. "She's got arthritis now. My vet says there's nothing we can do."

"Would you like the name of my vet? She's terrific."

"You've got a cat, too?"

"Oh, yes. She's the love of my life."

By now, all Maxine's resistance had melted away. I was a fellow cat lover.

"Come on in," she said. "I was just about to make some tea."

Still holding Sparkles, I followed Maxine into her apartment and looked around. The place was furnished in brown tweedy furniture, the kind of generic stuff you see at furniture rental places. I found it hard to believe that someone would actually go out and buy furniture this bland. It was like decorating your room with oatmeal.

"Make yourself comfortable," Maxine said. "I'll go put on the water for tea."

She scurried off to her kitchen, and I took a seat on an oatmeal sofa, still cradling Sparkles in my arms. The cat stared up at me worshipfully. Why couldn't Prozac ever give me some of this worshipful action?

Sparkles and I whiled away the next few minutes in a mutual lovefest until Maxine came back with a plate of Mallomars.

"Want one?" she asked, holding out the plate.

"Thanks," I said. "Mallomars are my favorite."

"Mine, too." She smiled shyly and sat down across from me in a muddy brown La-Z-Boy.

Sparkles wriggled free from my arms and slowly made her way over to Maxine, who picked her up, and settled her in her lap.

"Is my Sparkles comfy?" she cooed, in the same nauseating baby talk favored by cat lovers the world over.

"Such a tragedy about Frenchie," I said, getting down to the topic du jour.

"Yes," she echoed woodenly. "A tragedy."

Call me crazy, but this wasn't exactly the grief-stricken response I'd expected. Maxine had been Frenchie's only friend at Passions. Possibly her only friend, period. Shouldn't she be a tad more upset?

"Do you have any idea who might have killed her?"

"Well, you heard what Becky said about wanting to see Frenchie's corpse on the sales floor."

"You don't really think Becky is capable of murder, do you?"

"You'd be surprised at what some people are capable of," she said, rubbing Sparkles' belly with slow, even strokes. "I learned that the hard way."

"What do you mean?"

But she didn't get a chance to answer, because just then the tea kettle started shrieking.

"I'll be right back," she said, putting Sparkles down on the La-Z-Boy and heading for the kitchen.

Alone in the living room, I looked around for signs of a personal life and found nothing. No knickknacks.

No vacation souvenirs. No framed photos of loved ones. The room had about as much personality as a Motel 6.

I wandered over to a small oak bookshelf and scanned the books. Not much of interest. Just a few accounting books and some *Reader's Digest* Condensed Classics. I was about to return to the sofa when I noticed a brown leather volume stuck between two condensed classics. I pulled it out and saw that it was a photo album.

I brought it back to the sofa and started leafing through it. There weren't many pictures in the album: two formal portraits of a man and a woman, smiling stiffly at the camera, probably Maxine's parents. The rest were snapshots of Maxine as an awkward child, an awkward teenager, and an even more awkward adult.

Aside from Maxine and her parents, there were no other people in the book. Just a bunch of cats. Poor Maxine. What a lonely life she must have led. I was about to close the book and put it back on the shelf when a photo fluttered to the floor. It was a picture of Maxine at the beach, grinning into the camera. And for once, she wasn't alone. No, she stood arm in arm with Frenchie. At least I thought it was Frenchie. I recognized the Maltese cross on her chest. But I couldn't be sure, because her face and neck had been slashed beyond recognition.

"What do you think you're doing?"

I turned and saw Maxine. Her cheeks were flushed with anger.

"I was just looking at your photo album," I stammered. "I didn't think you'd mind."

"Well, I do," she said, snatching the mangled picture from me.

"The person with you in that picture," I said. "It's Frenchie, isn't it?"

"Yes, it's Frenchie." The bitterness in her voice was unmistakable.

"I don't understand. I thought you liked her."

"I did," she said. "Once."

She crumpled down into the La-Z-Boy. Sparkles meowed at her feet, too old and arthritic to make the leap into her lap.

"Want to tell me about it?" I asked.

She hesitated a beat. I smiled my most sympathetic smile. And I wasn't acting. At that moment, just thinking about that sad empty photo album, I really did feel sorry for her. I guess she must have decided she could trust me, because the next thing I knew, she was spilling her guts.

"I've never had many friends," she said, lifting Sparkles up into her lap. "So when Frenchie came to work at Passions and started asking me to join her for lunch, I was thrilled. Frenchie was everything I wasn't. Beautiful and confident and sophisticated. I couldn't believe she'd chosen me to be her friend. Before long, we weren't just having lunch together. We'd go out for dinners and movies, and sometimes we even went shopping together. For the first time in my life, I felt special."

She smiled at the memory.

"Then one night we were having dinner out at the beach, and Frenchie told me about her plan. It would be so easy, she said, to doctor Grace's account books and make it look like she'd been cheating on her taxes. Then Frenchie could use the doctored books to blackmail Grace into selling her the store. She said that Grace was old-fashioned, that she wasn't keeping up with the times. That it was only a matter of time before she ran Passions to the ground.

"At first I refused. No way was I going to do that to Grace. But Frenchie convinced me that I'd actually be doing Grace a favor. She told me that Grace had confided in her that she had a heart condition. Frenchie said that the stress of running the store could kill her.

"When I still hesitated, she said that once she took over the store, she'd double my salary. I must've been crazy, but I agreed to do it. Frenchie had this way about her; she could get me to do whatever she wanted."

I thought about Owen, and what he'd said about being under Frenchie's spell. Clearly he hadn't been the only one bewitched by her charms.

"I knew it wasn't right," Maxine said, "but I did it anyway. I stayed late at night and doctored the books. Grace never suspected anything, because I often work late. And then my part of the deal was done. Frenchie took over. She told Grace that unless she sold her the store for a nominal fee, she'd turn her over to the IRS for tax fraud. Grace was blindsided. She knew Frenchie had her over a barrel. She agreed to sell her the store for five dollars and announced her retirement. You were there that day. You saw how stunned she was.

"Afterward, I went to Frenchie's office to invite her to lunch. I'd made reservations at the Four Seasons to celebrate."

Then she winced, pained by what she was about to say.

"Frenchie looked at me like I was a cockroach that had wandered in from the sewer. She told me she wasn't going to have lunch with me that day. Or any day. She said she'd been bored to tears with me all along, that she couldn't wait to be rid of me. Not only was she not giving me a raise, she fired me. I couldn't believe my ears. She said that Grace didn't have a heart condition, that she was healthy as a horse. And that I was a gullible fool for believing her.

"I told her I'd report her to the police and she just laughed. She reminded me that I was the one who doctored the books, not her. She said that if anything happened to her, she'd make certain I was dragged down with her.

"Oh, Sparkles," she said, burying her face in the cat's fur. "How could I have been so foolish?"

Then she started to cry, big choking sobs that racked her thin body.

I hurried to her side and put my arm around her.

"You mustn't cry," I said. "Frenchie was a terrible person. You weren't a fool for believing her. You were just human."

She looked up at me with red-rimmed eyes.

"You're right," she said. "Frenchie *was* a terrible person. And you know something? I'm glad she's dead. But I didn't kill her. I swear I didn't."

"Just for the record, do you mind my asking where you were the night of the murder?"

"No, I don't mind. I was home that night. Sparkles and I were watching *The Way We Were*. It's one of our favorite movies. Right, Sparkles?"

Sparkles yawned. I guess she wasn't a Robert Redford fan.

"Well, I'd better get going," I said. "Thank you so much for your time."

I gave Maxine the name of my vet and she walked me to the door, still holding Sparkles in her arms.

"'Bye, Sparkles," I said, giving the cat one last scratch behind her ears.

Unwilling to venture onto the elevator from hell, I took the stairs, my footsteps echoing loudly in the empty stairwell. I couldn't help wondering if I'd just shared Mallomars with a killer.

True, mousy little Maxine didn't seem capable of murder. I wondered if she even had the strength to ram that shoe in Frenchie's neck. But it's amazing what people are capable of in moments of stress. Look at all those stories about ninety-eight-pound women lifting cars to rescue their children. I saw the way she'd mutilated Frenchie in her photo album. How could I be sure she hadn't unleashed her rage on her in real life, too?

Driving home from Maxine's, I had a sudden craving for roast chicken.

When I was a kid growing up in Hermosa Beach, Daddy cooked us roast chicken and mashed potatoes every Sunday night. Daddy is the cook in our family. He's really quite good, although he has a thing about washing vegetables. Which is why it's not uncommon to find a dollop of Palmolive Liquid in your mashed potatoes. But his chickens are delicious—crispy on the outside, juicy on the inside—and every once in a while I get a craving for one.

So I stopped off at Gelson's, glitzy supermarket to the stars, where you practically need a cosigner to shop, and picked out a glorious rosemary lemon chicken. Yes, I know that, given the state of my finances, I should've been shopping for discount chickens, but I was hungry and I didn't care.

I got in the car with my precious cargo and headed home. The aroma of roast chicken filled the Corolla. It was all I could do to keep myself from tearing into it at the first stoplight. But I restrained myself. I was determined to eat dinner the civilized way, at the dining room table, with a glass of chardonnay and Tony Bennett on the stereo.

"Look what Mommy brought for dinner, sweetie," I said to Prozac when I got home. "Yummy roast chicken."

She sniffed appreciatively and came hurrying to my side. She's very fond of me when I've got a chicken in my arms.

"Don't worry. I'll cut you a nice big piece."

She meowed noisily. *White meat only*, was what I think she was trying to tell me.

I put the chicken on the counter and poured myself a glass of chardonnay. Then I set the table with a placemat and cloth napkin and put Tony on the stereo. I really had to do this civilized stuff more often.

I thought briefly of relaxing with my drink before dinner, like civilized types do, but I simply couldn't resist the smell of that chicken.

I was just about to tear off the wrapping when the phone rang. I raced to the living room to get it. If it was a telemarketer, I'd scream bloody murder.

A stranger's voice came on the line.

"Hi, it's Darrell Simms."

Damn. It *was* a telemarketer.

"Whatever you're selling, I don't want any."

"I'm not selling anything. We met the other night. At speed dating. Remember? I was the one who liked boating."

I vaguely remembered some guy blathering on endlessly about his boat.

"How did you get my number?"

"From the speed dating people. I was one of the guys you said yes to."

But I hadn't said yes to anyone, as those of you paying attention will surely remember. Those idiots at speed dating must have given out my number by mistake.

"Anyhow," he said, "I was wondering if you'd like to get together and go for a sunset sail on my boat."

I was just about to say no when I flashed on the image of Maxine sitting in her oatmeal recliner with Sparkles on her lap. Did I really want to wind up like her, a sad, lonely lady with only a cat for company? Here was a perfectly nice guy asking me to go sailing. On a sunset cruise. How sweet was that? So what if he'd seemed a tad boring the other night? Maybe he was nervous. Kandi was right. I couldn't let my disastrous marriage to The Blob turn me off men forever. I had to start giving guys a chance.

"Sounds great," I said.

We agreed to meet Sunday at 4:00 at the marina, and I hung up, feeling quite proud of myself. In addition to being more civilized, I had to start opening myself up to new adventures. And maybe lose ten pounds while I was at it. But I'd worry about those ten pounds later. Right now, I had a roast chicken to demolish.

I was just heading back to the kitchen when the phone rang again.

Isn't that always the way it is? When you're in the middle of a writing assignment and you're totally blocked and you'd give a million dollars to be interrupted by a call, the phone refuses to ring. But just have a roast chicken on your kitchen counter, and you're more popular than a blue-eyed blonde in a sports bar.

"Yes," I barked. "Who is it?"

"Don't bite my head off. It's me. Kandi."

"Kandi, the strangest thing just happened. One of the speed dating guys called and asked me out. I guess they must have given out my number by mistake."

There was silence on the line.

"Kandi? Are you still there?"

"Yeah, I'm here. Actually, the people at speed dating didn't give out your phone number. I did."

"What?"

"When you went to the ladies' room, I changed all your no's to yeses."

"Why would you do that? You said all the guys were losers."

"I did not say they were losers. I said they were goofballs."

"Losers. Goofballs. Whatever. Why did you give them my number?"

"I figured in your case, a goofball was better than nothing."

"What do you mean, *in my case?*"

"I just wanted you to get out of the house, that's all. You spend way too much time with Prozac."

"I do not," I said, plucking cat hairs from my bra.

"Besides," Kandi said, "even though they all *seemed* like goofballs, that doesn't mean they really *are* goofballs. It was only three minutes per guy, for heaven's sake. We didn't really get a chance to know them."

I had to admit, she had a point. But I was still pretty annoyed. For all she knew, one of those guys could be a goofball mass murderer. And I was just about to give her a serious scolding when I heard my call waiting beep.

"Look, I've got another call. I'll yell at you later, okay?"

I switched to the other call. It was Becky.

"Oh, Jaine. I've got bad news. The police have a

witness who saw my car parked outside Passions the night of the murder."

"But that's impossible. You weren't there."

"Actually," she said, somewhat sheepishly, "I was there. I went back to get my dress designs. I'd given some of them to Grace. I was afraid Frenchie might not give them back to me, so I went back around seven o'clock. The store was closed by then, and I figured Frenchie would be gone.

"Now some guy says he saw my car in the parking lot. Only he swears it was there later that night, about ten-thirty. And the cops say Frenchie was murdered some time between nine and eleven."

"How can the police be so sure that it was your car in the parking lot? Did the witness write down the license plate number?"

"My car's pretty easy to identify. It's an orange Beetle. I got it to match my hair. The license plate says 'Becky's Bug'."

Oh, great. She might as well have left a business card.

"Who is this witness, anyway?" I asked.

"All I know is that the cops said he lives above the store next door to Passions. Oh, Jaine. What are we going to do?"

Her voice was screechy with panic.

"Do you have anything you can take to relax? A valium, maybe?"

"I've got some Sleepy Time Herbal Tea."

Sleepy Time Herbal Tea? That was the strongest sedative she had, in a town where people pop mind-altering drugs like M&Ms?

"Okay, try that," I said. "I'll check in with you tomorrow."

I assured Becky that everything was going to be okay and got off the phone. But I was lying. I sincerely doubted everything was going to be okay. Not with an eyewitness who placed Becky's car at Passions at the time of the murder. Surely, the guy got the time wrong. First thing tomorrow, I'd track him down and have a talk with him.

In the meantime, though, I had a chicken to eat.

Taking no chances, I took the phone off the hook and made a beeline for my roast chicken. I couldn't wait to dig in.

But Prozac, the little monster, had beaten me to it. There she was on the counter, her pink nose buried in the white meat.

"Prozac!" I wailed. "How could you?"

It was easy, she seemed to say, licking her lips. *In case you've forgotten, I'm very good at jumping up on counters.*

I grabbed the bird and surveyed the damage. It's amazing how much chicken a ten-pound cat can eat. For a minute I considered eating what was left. But as hungry as I was, I couldn't bring myself to eat a chicken covered with cat spit.

I wrapped the remains and put them in the refrigerator. They'd be leftovers for Prozac, although Lord knows she didn't deserve them.

Then I fixed myself a bowl of Cheerios, which I ate standing over the kitchen sink.

So much for the civilized life.

YOU'VE GOT MAIL

To: Jausten
From: Shoptillyoudrop
Subject: Your Father Is Impossible!

Well, rehearsals have started and all I can say is: Your father is impossible! I swear, he's driving everyone crazy. He has one measly line: *Very good, sir.* But he refuses to say it. Instead, he keeps making up his own dialogue. He says, "Anything you say, sir." "Your wish is my command, sir." "Indubitably, sir." Anything but "Very good, sir."

And every gesture he does with a flourish. He practically does a backflip when he opens the door. In one scene he's supposed to light Alistair's cigarette. He makes such a production over it, waving the lighter like it's a baton. By the time he finally lights the darn cigarette, Alistair could have already smoked it.

The worst part is when Alistair and I have our love scene. We don't really kiss, of course. We just fake it. But every time Alistair comes near me, your father starts coughing and shooting Alistair dirty looks. Oh, honey, it's just so embarrassing. Daddy is convinced Alistair has a crush on me. All because he sent me those roses. As it turns out, Alistair sent flowers to *all* the ladies in the play. But still, your daddy is convinced that Alistair has "the hots" for me. Which is totally absurd. Our relationship is strictly professional!

Your stressed out,
Mom

To: Jausten
From: DaddyO
Subject: A Wolf in Wolf's Clothing

Can you believe the gall of The Germ sending your
mother a dozen roses? True, he sent flowers to the
other women in the cast, but he sent them *carnations*!
What does that tell you, huh? The man is a wolf in
wolf's clothing.

And you wouldn't believe the fuss your mother is
making over that damn bouquet. You'd think she never
got any flowers before. Didn't I just give her a dozen
gorgeous roses last Mother's Day?

To: DaddyO
From: Jausten

Actually, Daddy, I think you gave her a dustbuster.

To: Jausten
From: DaddyO
Subject: It's the Thought That Counts

Really? I could've sworn I sent her roses. Oh, well.
It's the thought that counts. And besides, when I *do*
give your mother roses, I give her good ones. Not the
puny little buds The Germ sent. I bet they don't last a
day.

To: Jausten
From: Shoptillyoudrop

P.S. Daddy did something to those roses, I'm sure of
it. They're wilting already. He swears he went
nowhere near them, but I think I smell gin in the vase.

Chapter 15

The store next to Passions was a hair salon called Extreme Hair. And they weren't kidding. The window was filled with pictures of gaunt young models with what looked like antelope horns on their heads. I don't care what the folks at Extreme Hair say, it's not a good idea to walk around with antelope horns on your head. Especially during hunting season.

But I wasn't there to critique haircuts. I was there to pay a call on the witness who'd seen Becky's car on the night of the murder. Luckily there was only one apartment above the salon. The name on the mailbox was R.D. Butler.

I headed up a narrow flight of steps and rang the bell to R.D.'s apartment. A skinny young guy opened the door. His greasy blond hair was braided in dreadlocks that stuck out from his head like spikes. An Extreme Hair customer, no doubt. He wore nothing but pajama bottoms, exposing a painfully thin chest studded with nipple rings.

I wondered if R.D. stood for Really Dirty.

"Whaddaya want?" he said, peering out at me with bloodshot eyes.

"I hope I didn't wake you," I said.

"You sure did," he snapped.

"Sorry about that. I was wondering if I could ask you a few questions about the murder next door."

"I already told the police everything I know. What are you—some kind of reporter?" He squinted at me appraisingly. "You *are* a reporter, aren't you? From the *L.A. Times,* I'll bet."

I was just about to assure him that no, I wasn't a pesky reporter, when he said: "I'll talk to you on one condition. You make sure you mention the name of my band in the paper."

"Absolutely," I nodded. "No problem. I'll be sure to mention your band's name."

"Okay," he said, scratching his scalp between the dreadlocks. "We got a deal. Come on in."

It's a good thing I wasn't from the Board of Health, or his apartment would have been condemned on the spot. What a pigsty. The place was practically buried in beer cans, fast food wrappers, and petrified pizza crusts.

I plucked what looked like a decomposing egg roll from a chair and sat down, making a mental note to have my jeans fumigated.

"My sources tell me that you're a witness in the Giselle Ambrose murder case," I said, doing my best to sound like a reporter.

"That's right," R.D. said, scratching his underarms.

"Can you tell me what you witnessed?"

"Dead Bats."

"Dead bats?"

"That's the name of my band. Aren't you going to write that down?"

"No need," I said, tapping my forehead. "Photographic memory."

"Really? That's great. I have trouble remembering my phone number."

"You should try laying off cocaine. I hear that helps."

Of course, I didn't really say that. What I said was: "So what did you see the night of the murder?"

"Like I told the cops, at 10:35, I saw an orange VW Beetle out in the parking lot."

"You sure of the time?"

"Yeah, I'm sure. I was sleeping off a hangover and got up to pee. I happened to look out the window and saw the Beetle. Then I checked the clock over there."

He pointed to a big round neon clock hanging over the sofa, the kind you see in diners. I wondered if he'd stolen it.

"I remember it was 10:35," he said. "Exactly."

This from a guy who had trouble remembering his phone number.

"Were there any other cars there? Like maybe a BMW?"

"I didn't see a BMW."

My heart leapt. If he didn't see a Beemer, then Frenchie couldn't have been there, and Becky couldn't have murdered her.

"But that doesn't mean it wasn't there," he added.

"What do you mean?"

"Come here by the window, and I'll show you."

I tiptoed through the trash and looked down at Passions' parking lot.

"You have to be standing right here at the window to see the cars parked directly below, under those jacaranda trees," R.D. said. "But if you're standing in the middle of the room, like I was that night, you can't see these cars. All I could see were the cars parked at the far side of the lot. So another car could've been here."

I plopped back down in the egg-roll chair, disappointed, and watched as R.D. began rummaging through some papers on his coffee table.

"Here it is," he said, handing me a piece of paper. "Our schedule."

"What schedule?"

"For the band. Our gigs."

I glanced down at the paper he handed me.

"This is a pizza take-out menu."

"Sorry, I don't see so hot without my contacts."

"You wear contact lenses?"

"Yeah."

"Were you wearing them the other night when you saw the orange Beetle?"

"No. But I know I saw that car."

"I'm sure you did."

But here's the thing: Without his contacts, he could have easily gotten the time wrong. He swore he saw the car at 10:35. But what if—groggy with sleep and without his contacts—he'd seen the hands on the clock reversed? What if, instead of 10:35, it was five of seven?

"Here, I found the schedule." He handed me another piece of paper, this time a menu from The Falafel Palace.

"Great," I said, heading for the door.

"You won't forget to mention us?"

"Nope. The Dead Rats are going to be page-one news."

"Dead Bats."

"Right. Dead Bats."

R.D.'s eyes narrowed to suspicious slits.

"Wait a minute. I thought you said you had a photographic memory."

"Guess it went out of focus for a minute. Well, gotta run. Important story breaking at City Hall."

Before he could reply, I left him scratching his armpits and scooted out the door.

If my theory was right, Becky was nowhere near Passions at the time of the murder. Now all I had to do was find out who *was* there, and I'd catch myself a killer.

Back downstairs, the stylists at Extreme Hair were busy maiming hair. I silently offered their victims my condolences and headed next door to Passions to have a talk with Grace Lynbrook. Of all my suspects, it seemed that Grace had the most to gain by Frenchie's death.

Becky and Tyler were both busy with customers when I walked in the door. Becky gave me a faint smile. Her skin was pale and mottled, and the dark circles under her eyes were a sure sign that she hadn't had much sleep.

I waved to her and headed back to Grace's office. The door was open, and I could see Mrs. Tucker, the recycled teenager, sitting across the desk from Grace in one of Grace's white wicker chairs. Bessie the mannequin, I was happy to see, was still in her place, propped up against the wall. In spite of Frenchie's threat to toss her in the Dumpster, Bessie had survived Frenchie's reign of terror intact, except for one of her arms, which had fallen off and was lying on the floor at the hem of her bell-bottoms.

"See, Grace?" Mrs. Tucker was saying. "I told you everything would work out." She looked down at her watch. "Oh, dear. I'm late for my botox shots." She shot up from the wicker chair. "Gotta run, sweetie. I'll call you later." She blew her a kiss, then headed out the back door to the parking lot.

I waited a few seconds, then poked my head in the door.

"Jaine!" Grace shot me a bright smile. "Come on in, and have a seat."

She looked about 300 times better than the day she "retired." Her eyes shone brightly, and unlike poor Becky, she was brimming with good cheer.

I sat down in the chair recently vacated by Mrs. Tucker. I could smell her perfume, one of those overwhelming scents that give people asthma attacks in elevators.

"Jaine, dear," Grace said. "I'm afraid I won't be needing your services any more." She pointed to the *Los Angeles Times* on her desk. "We're getting all the publicity we can handle right now."

And it's true. The story had been front-page news for days.

"Actually," I said, "that's not why I'm here."

"Oh?"

"I wanted to talk to you about Frenchie's murder."

"Such a terrible tragedy," she tsk-tsked, with an impressive lack of feeling.

"Did you know that the police suspect Becky?" I asked.

"No, I didn't. That's terrible. Becky's not a murderer."

"That's why I'm investigating on her behalf, to try and find the real killer."

"Don't tell me you're a private eye?" Her eyes widened with disbelief.

"Part-time," I nodded.

"But don't you have to be in shape to do that kind of work?"

Ouch.

Amazing as it may seem, I felt like telling her, *I've managed to solve a case or two in my queen-size panty-hose.*

She must've sensed I was irritated.

"Sorry. I didn't mean to insult you. It's just that all the private eyes on TV are so incredibly buff."

"Everybody on TV is buff. It's part of the wonderful world of make-believe."

She smiled wryly. "You've got a point there.

"So," she said, clasping her hands on her desk, "how can I help you?"

"You can start by telling me if you have any idea who could've killed Frenchie."

"Not a clue." She went back to her tsk-tsk schtick. "Poor Frenchie. I was so very fond of her. She was a real asset to the store."

She tried her best to look sincere, but it didn't work. She may have once been a model, but she sure as hell wasn't an actress.

"Look," I said, cutting to the chase, "I know that Frenchie was blackmailing you. Maxine told me how she forced you to sell the store to her. Maxine told me everything." Accent on *everything.*

Suddenly all her phony grief vanished.

"All right," she said, tossing back her snowy hair. "It's true. Frenchie forced me to sell her the store. Thankfully, she got killed before we could sign the final papers, so the store was still in my name at the time of her death."

"I hate to say it, but you had a pretty strong motive to kill her." I didn't really hate to say it, not after that crack about my being out of shape. "Some people might figure that you killed her to get your store back."

"Some people would be wrong. I'll grant you that I

was in a state of shock at first. But after I thought about it, I decided I wasn't going to give up without a fight. I was planning to go to the police and tell them what Frenchie had done. After all, she was the one who broke the law, not me. It was extortion pure and simple, and she undoubtedly would've wound up in jail. So you see, even though I can't say I'm sorry Frenchie's dead, I didn't kill her."

If she was acting now, she was doing a damn good job.

"Do you mind my asking where you were on the night of the murder?"

"Not at all. I was having a late dinner with a friend."

I took a stab in the dark.

"That friend wouldn't happen to be Mrs. Tucker, would it?"

"As a matter of fact, it is. Amanda and I have been friends for years."

"So you didn't come back to the store that night?"

Her smile stiffened. I'd hit a nerve.

"I only ask," I said, "because I happened to notice those jacaranda blossoms stuck to the roof of your car. If you recall, it was raining the night of the murder, and you know how sticky jacaranda blossoms are in the rain. They're practically like glue."

"No," she said, her smile now frozen on her face. "I was nowhere near the store the night of the murder. Just ask Mrs. Tucker if you don't believe me. Now if you'll excuse me, I've got work to do."

She put on a pair of steel-rimmed granny glasses and began shuffling papers on her desk. Class dismissed.

It looked like I wouldn't be writing any ads for Grace Lynbrook in my lifetime.

I headed out to the sales floor, lost in thought. I'd be willing to bet a month's rent that Grace had been at Passions the night of the murder. True, that didn't mean she killed Frenchie. She might have gone back to get something, like Becky did. Maybe she wanted one of her wicker chairs, or a souvenir pair of spandex bike shorts.

Then again, it was very possible that she did kill her. Maybe she didn't really have dinner with Mrs. Tucker. Maybe Mrs. Tucker was prepared to lie for her. Or maybe it was Grace who was lying for Mrs. Tucker. For all I knew, they were in it together. Maybe they drove over in Grace's car, stabbed Frenchie in the neck with her Jimmy Choo knockoff, then went back home to share a brandy.

I definitely needed to have a chat with Mrs. Amanda Tucker.

Back on the sales floor, Tyler was folding tank tops, and Becky was ringing up a customer. I waited till she was free, then hustled to her side. Up close, the dark circles under her eyes were even more noticeable.

"Hi, Jaine," she smiled wearily. "How's it going?"

"Great," I assured her with false bravado. "I'm making lots of progress on the case."

"Really?" she asked, brightening.

No, but I wasn't going to tell her that.

"Do you think you could get me Mrs. Tucker's address and phone number?"

"No problem," she said. "I'm sure she's here in our guest book." She rifled through the pages of a guest book on the counter. "Here it is. Amanda Tucker. First on the list."

She copied the information on the back of a Passions business card.

"Thanks," I said, slipping the card into my purse. "Now try to get some sleep tonight. Everything's going to be fine. I promise."

Then I hugged her and walked out the door, hoping I'd be able to live up to my promise.

Chapter 16

I was heading for the parking lot when I heard, "Jaine! Wait up!" I turned and saw Tyler hurrying after me. Like Grace, he looked a hell of a lot better than the last time I saw him.

"I was just going to grab a hot dog at Pink's," he said. "Want to join me?"

The last thing my intestinal tract needed was another gutful of chili cheese dogs. But I didn't want to pass up this opportunity to talk to Tyler. He was, after all, one of my suspects.

"Sure," I said. "Sounds great."

Ten minutes later, we were seated outside at Pink's, scarfing down chili cheese dogs and fries. Tyler ate his hot dog with gusto, wiping the chili sauce from his mouth with the back of his hand. Even with grease dripping down his arm, the guy was incredibly attractive.

"I love these things," he said. "But I feel guilty eating them when Becky's around. She's right about eating animals. It's pretty awful when you think about it, but I can't seem to give it up."

"Just keep telling yourself they died of natural causes. That's what I always do."

"I've got to try that sometime," he said, flashing me a heart-melting grin. I could just imagine how many women he'd turned to mush with that one.

Then the grin disappeared.

"I'm worried about Becky," he said. "I've never seen her this upset."

"I'd be upset, too, if the cops suspected me of murder."

"She told me you're investigating the case."

"That's true," I nodded.

"Funny, I'd never in a million years guess you were a private eye."

Amazing, isn't it, how everyone assumed I couldn't solve my way out of a crossword puzzle?

"So who do you think did it?" he asked.

"It's too early to tell," I said, thinking it might possibly be Tyler. Sure, he seemed like a nice guy, but so did Ted Bundy. And I'd seen that murderous look in his eyes when he had his hands around Frenchie's neck. He'd said he wanted to kill her, and in fact, he almost did. Maybe he came back later that night to finish the job.

"I hope you won't be offended," I said, licking the last of the chili sauce from my fingers, "but where were you the night of the murder?"

"I'm not offended. Not at all. Detectives have to suspect everybody, right? Otherwise they're not doing their job."

"So where were you that night?"

"Actually I was at my writing course at UCLA."

I'd taken night courses at UCLA, and I knew they ended about ten. Becky said Frenchie'd been killed some time between nine and eleven. Which meant

Tyler could have easily driven over to Passions and done the dirty deed.

"The class broke up around ten," he said, as if reading my thoughts, "but I stayed afterward to have a conference with my writing instructor. Ms. Garrett's been a real mentor to me. She's great with all her students. Last year, one of her students sold a book to Random House and dedicated it to her. Anyhow, Ms. Garrett could tell how upset I was, so she stayed after class to help me put things in perspective. She got me to see that it was only my novel that was destroyed, not my life. We worked on reconstructing the outline and were there till close to midnight."

I stared at a dollop of chili sauce on his chin, and suddenly I had an irresistible urge to reach over and wipe it off. I didn't, of course, but there was something about Tyler that brought out the maternal instinct in me.

Frankly, I was glad he had an alibi.

"Look," he said, "for a crazy moment, I really did want to kill Frenchie. After all, she'd destroyed three years of hard work. But I didn't do it. Honest. Besides, things aren't nearly as bleak as they seemed at first. Ms. Garrett still has copies of chapters that I submitted to her in class. Between those chapters and my outline, eventually I'll be able to piece the book together again."

He looked at me with such open, trusting eyes that it suddenly seemed absurd to suspect him of murder.

"If there's anything I can do to get Becky out of this mess," he said, "just let me know. I hate seeing her like this."

"Do you have any idea who might have done it?" I asked.

He shrugged. "My money's on Grace. She seems nice on the outside, but there's a cold streak in her. I

wouldn't put it past her. Especially since she had so
much to gain by Frenchie's death."

Exactly what I'd been thinking.

"Here's my card," I said. "In case you think of anything that might help. You can contact me anytime. Day
or night."

"Absolutely," he said, putting my card in his wallet.

We finished our dogs and started walking back to
Passions. I was grateful for the exercise. By the time we
got back, I figured I'd burned off at least a hundred chili
cheese dog calories.

Great. A hundred down. Only eight zillion more
to go.

As we approached Passions' parking lot, we saw
Becky coming out the back door.

"Hey, Beck," Tyler said. "Where are you off to?"

"Grace wants me to get her car washed."

No doubt to get rid of those incriminating jacaranda
blossoms.

"I'll be back soon," she said, giving Tyler a peck on
the lips. "Wait a minute. Is that a chili cheese dog I
smell on your breath?"

Tyler grinned sheepishly. "Guilty as charged."

"I wish you wouldn't use that expression," Becky
said, wincing. "I'm afraid I'm going to be hearing it in
a courtroom one of these days."

"Don't be silly," Tyler said. "Everything's going to
be fine. Jaine's going to find the killer. Isn't that right,
Jaine?"

I nodded weakly, wishing I shared his confidence.

Tyler hugged Becky, one of those hugs that, had I not
been there, might have easily led to some hanky-panky.

But I was there, so he reluctantly broke away and headed back into the store.

"Does Grace often ask you to get her car washed?" I asked, as Becky and I walked to Grace's Jaguar.

"Yes, but usually on Mondays. For some reason, though, she wanted me to do it today."

I knew the reason, and it was called destroying evidence.

"I hate driving her Jag," Becky said. "I'm always afraid I'll get into an accident. Now where did I put the keys?"

She began rummaging through her purse, a large felt bag shaped like a monkey.

"Interesting handbag," I said.

"Thanks," she said. "I designed it myself."

Only a sprite like Becky could get away with wearing a monkey on her arm.

"Oh, here they are." She pulled out the car keys, and as she did, something clattered to the pavement.

I looked down and saw Frenchie's Maltese cross.

"Oh, gosh," Becky said, quickly snatching it up. "I forgot I had this in my purse."

Then I guess she must have noticed my gaping jaw.

"This doesn't look good, does it?" she said.

"No, it doesn't. Do you mind my asking how you got it?"

"I found it on the sink in the ladies' room a few days before the murder. Frenchie used the ladies' room at Passions to change outfits before she went out on her dates. Anyhow, I saw it on the sink, and I don't know what came over me, but I took it. I knew Frenchie'd stolen it, and I'd be darned if I was going to let her keep it."

"What did you intend to do with it?" I asked.

"I wasn't sure. I thought maybe I'd try to track down the customer she'd stolen it from. Or maybe I'd turn it over to Grace. All I knew was that I didn't want Frenchie to have it. So I put it in my purse. And then, what with the murder and everything, I forgot all about it."

Her eyes widened with fear.

"If the cops find out I've got Frenchie's necklace, they'll think I killed her for sure. Oh, Jaine. What am I going to do?"

Then I did something very foolish.

"Give it to me," I said.

She handed it to me and I slipped it into my pocket.

"I'll keep it until this whole thing blows over."

"Oh, thank you, Jaine," she said, throwing her arms around me. "You're an angel!"

Then she climbed into Grace's Jag and drove off, clutching the steering wheel with white knuckles, her absurd monkey handbag on the seat beside her.

It wasn't until I was halfway home that I realized just how foolish I'd been.

What if Becky had been lying to me? What if, in spite of her childlike appearance, she was a cold-blooded killer? What if she'd taken Frenchie's Maltese cross from around her neck right after she'd stabbed said neck in the jugular? Had the cops zeroed in on the right suspect after all?

But then why had Becky hired me to investigate? Maybe she thought I was such an incompetent dufus that I'd nail the wrong person. Or maybe she was so deep in denial-land, she'd convinced herself she was innocent. Maybe she honestly thought there was a "real killer" out there.

Guilty or innocent, one thing was certain: I'd been

an idiot to take the necklace. At the very least, I could be arrested for withholding evidence. At worst, I could be arrested for aiding and abetting a criminal.

By the time I drove up to my duplex, I was a nervous wreck. I couldn't wait to pour myself a glass of chardonnay.

But as luck would have it, I couldn't find a parking space. That's the trouble with my apartment. It's got plenty of charm, but no parking. I drove around for what seemed like hours, until I finally found a spot.

I parked the Corolla and headed for my duplex, fingering the gold pendant in my pocket like a bad luck charm. At one point, I took it out and checked it for dried blood. I didn't see any, but that didn't mean anything. Becky would've washed it away by now.

Finally I got home and poured myself a glass of chardonnay. By the time I'd finished it, I felt a lot better. Surely, Becky wasn't a killer. I'd overreacted, that's all. I'd go on with my investigation and find the real killer and have a good laugh over how scared I'd been.

But just to play it safe, I hid the Maltese cross in a pair of hot pink sequinned mules my mom had bought me from the Home Shopping Channel. She ordered them to go with the hot pink sequinned capri's and tank top she'd also sent me. Over the years, I've tried to tell my mom I'm a writer, not a hooker, but she still insists on sending me these outrageous outfits. But that's a whole other story, one I intend to share with a therapist, as soon as I can afford one.

In the meanwhile, though, I had a murder to solve. So I put in a call to the sad-eyed detective in charge of the case, whose name, according to his business card, was Lt. Frank Mula.

Luckily, he was in when I called.

"Lt. Mula," I said, "this is Jaine Austen."

"Right. And I'm Charles Dickens."

"Don't you remember? I'm the one who found the body at Passions."

"Oh, right. Sorry about that. How're you doing?"

"Fine. In fact, I've got some information that might be of help to you."

"Actually, we've got a pretty good handle on the case."

"That's great," I said. "But I think you're really going to be interested in what I've got to say."

"Okay," he said, not exactly bubbling with enthusiasm. "What is it?"

I told him how I'd visited his star witness, R.D. Butler, and how R.D. was blind as a bat without his contacts, and how he could have easily gotten the time wrong when he saw Becky's car in the parking lot.

"Very interesting," he said, not sounding the least bit interested. In fact, I could've sworn I heard him stifling a yawn.

Then I told him about the jacaranda blossoms on the roof of Grace Lynbrook's car, and how they must've got stuck there in the rain, and how the only night it had rained in the past two weeks was the night of the murder.

"So you see," I said, feeling quite Sherlock Holmesian, "I'm pretty sure Grace Lynbrook was at Passions the night of the murder."

I sat back and waited for him to be bowled over by my powers of deduction.

I waited in vain.

"What are you?" Lt. Mula asked. "Some kind of detective?"

"As a matter of fact, I am."

"I thought you were a writer."

"I am. I do the detecting part-time."

"Funny, I never would have figured you for a private dick."

If one more person said that, I'd scream.

"So what do you think of my jacaranda-in-the-rain theory?"

"I'll have our guys in forensic meteorology check it out."

"Forensic meteorology? I've never heard of that before. Is there really such a thing?"

"No, not really," he said, with a most annoying chuckle. "A little cop humor."

Harty har har. Très amusing.

"Thanks for the input," he said. "I'll look into it. But I've got to go now. Important call coming in."

Before I could reply, he clicked me off the line. At least, he thought he clicked me off the line. But unbeknownst to him, I was still there.

"Hey, Eddie," I heard him say. "We on for bowling tonight?"

I slammed down the receiver in disgust.

Lt. Mula wasn't going to be looking into any of my theories. He'd obviously written me off as an incompetent amateur.

I'd just have to prove him wrong, wouldn't I?

Fifteen minutes later, I was up to my earlobes in bubbles.

I'd retreated to the bathtub to think about the case. I do some of my best thinking in the tub. That's where I thought of my highly successful slogan for The Ackerman Awning Company: *Just a Shade Better.* Hey, it's not Shakespeare, but it pays the rent.

So there I was, lying in the tub, loofa-ing my thighs while I tried to figure out who killed Frenchie Ambrose.

Grace Lynbrook sure had the motive. And I couldn't rule out Maxine, not with that mutilated photo of Frenchie in her photo album. There was Frenchie's husband, Owen, who for all I knew could have been faking those tears of grief. And what about Grace's buddy, Amanda Tucker? I remembered what she'd said to Grace, that she knew all along that Grace would get her store back. Just how had she been so sure, unless she'd had a hand in getting rid of Frenchie?

"What do you think?" I asked Prozac, who was perched on top of the toilet tank. "Who's our killer?"

But Prozac was too busy licking her genitals to participate in the conversation.

I reached for the legal pad and pencil I'd brought to the tub and started to make notes. I always find it helps to write things out when I've got a problem to solve. I'd gotten as far as . . .

My Suspects
by Jaine Austen

. . . when the doorbell rang.

Who on earth could that be? Maybe it was Lance, back from the dry cleaners with my Prada suit.

I hauled myself out of the tub, and into my bathrobe.

"Lance?" I said, hurrying to the door. "Is that you?"

"No, ma'am. It's the police."

The police? Damn. They'd probably been tailing Becky and saw her giving me the Maltese cross. And now they were going to arrest me for aiding and abetting a criminal!

"Just a minute," I called out. I hurried into the bedroom and threw on a pair of sweats. By the time I opened the front door to the two Beverly Hills cops on my front step, I was in an advanced state of panic.

I took a deep breath and forced myself to calm down. As long as they couldn't find the cross, the cops had no proof that I had it in my possession. I'd just have to play it cool.

I plastered a phony smile on my face.

"Can I help you, officers?" I said, my voice a terrified squeak. So much for cool.

"Yes, ma'am," one of them said, "you can."

Just remember, I told myself. *Admit nothing. As long as they can't find the cross, you're safe.*

And then to my horror I saw Prozac sashaying into the living room, a hot pink sequinned mule in her mouth.

I stood there, frozen to the spot, as she pranced over to the cops, the mule dangling from her mouth.

Look what I brought you, she seemed to be saying. *An ugly shoe.*

Oh, God, I prayed, please let it be the mule without the cross.

No such luck.

Prozac dropped the shoe at the cops' feet and the cross came tumbling out.

"I know I shouldn't have done it!" I wailed, going from cool to coward in record time. (Remind me never to get a job as an international spy.)

"That's right," one of the cops said. "You shouldn't have."

"I don't know what came over me."

"That's not much of an excuse," the other cop said, shaking his head.

"I suppose you're going to arrest me," I said, already picturing myself sharing a jail cell with a woman named Big Pete.

The cops exchanged puzzled looks.

"We don't usually arrest people for illegal parking, ma'am."

"Huh?" I blinked, puzzled.

"You own a white Corolla, right?"

"That's right."

"You parked it illegally in front of a driveway."

Was that it? They were here because I'd parked in a driveway? There was a God, after all!

"We got a call from the homeowner, and you've got him blocked in. You've got to move your car. And we're going to have to give you a ticket."

"That's all right, officer. I don't mind. Only sixty dollars? What a bargain."

And it was true. For the first time in my life, I was actually thrilled to get a ticket.

After reparking the Corolla, I headed back to my apartment, where I found Prozac, the little traitor, howling for her dinner. She looked up at me with innocent green eyes, as if she hadn't just tried to sell me down the river.

"You don't deserve this," I said, tossing her a bowl of Fancy Fish Entrails.

Then I stashed the Maltese cross in my sock drawer, threw my aborted suspect list in the trash, and climbed into bed with some Progresso Minestrone, which I ate straight from the can. I'd had enough detecting for one day.

I spent the rest of the night watching an Andy Hardy film festival on TV. By the time the last movie rolled around (*Andy Hardy Has Prostate Problems*), Andy was middle aged and I was exhausted. So I turned out the light and called it a day.

The last thing I remember before drifting off to sleep was Prozac curling up in the crook of my neck, breathing Fancy Fish Entrails in my face.

YOU'VE GOT MAIL

To: Jausten
From: Shoptillyoudrop
Subject: Calm before the Storm

Oh, dear. You'll never guess what happened! Alistair's
been in touch with a reporter from the *Tampa Tribune*
who's doing a story on local community theater. He
wants to see our play, but he's working under a dead-
line. So Alistair's pushed up our opening. Believe it or
not, we're going on stage with *Lord Worthington's
Ascot* in just two days. Good heavens, I'm a nervous
wreck! Not only do I have to learn all my lines, but I
have to learn them with a British accent!

And Daddy hasn't made things any easier, what with
all his crazy shenanigans. Although he seems to have
calmed down in the past few days. He's stopped making up his own dialogue and coughing during the love
scenes.

And yet, somehow I don't trust him. It's like the calm
before the storm. I just know he's up to something. I
can feel it in my bones.

To: Shoptillyoudrop
From: Jausten

Don't worry, Mom. I'm sure Daddy realized how
badly he was behaving and has turned over a new leaf.
Just go out there on opening night, and knock 'em
dead!

To: DaddyO
From: Jausten

Mom thinks you're up to something. Are you?

To: Jausten
From: DaddyO

Who? Moi?

Chapter 17

The sun was streaming in my bedroom window when I woke up the next morning. It was an impossibly beautiful day, with a sky as blue as a starlet's eyes. Whatever doubts I'd had about Becky's innocence had vanished in the night. I simply could not believe she was capable of murder.

So it was with a great sense of relief that I headed to the kitchen to fix breakfast.

"Here you go, Prozac," I said, tossing her a bowl of pink mush. "Yummy shrimp guts."

I stared into my Mother Hubbard-ish cupboards, wondering what I could scrape up for my breakfast. I was debating between a stale Pop Tart and a stale bagel when the doorbell rang.

It was Lance.

"Look what I brought," he said, holding out two paper sacks. "French roast coffee and croissants still warm from the bakery. With butter. And strawberry jam."

Why are all the good ones always gay?

Three minutes later, we were sitting at my dining room table, watching the butter melt on our croissants.

"I've got good news for you," Lance said. "The cleaners think they can get out the wine stains from your Prada suit."

"Oh, Lance. That's wonderful!"

I would've thrown my arms around him and hugged him, but I couldn't tear myself away from my croissant.

"So tell me all about your investigation," Lance said. "Do you have any idea who did it?"

"Not really. But I've got plenty of promising suspects."

I ran down my list of suspects, filling him in on the jacaranda blossoms on Grace's car; the mutilated head in Maxine's photo album; Frenchie's cuckolded husband, Owen; and Grace's good buddy and possible partner in crime, Mrs. Amanda Tucker.

"I didn't know Amanda Tucker was a friend of Grace's," Lance said, reaching for another croissant. I'd long since finished my second and was working on my third.

"Do you know her?" I asked.

"Not personally, but I see her picture in the society pages all the time. The woman has had her face tightened so many times, I'm surprised she can still close her eyes."

"Know anything about her?"

"Just that she's got money up her kazoo. Her husband was a billionaire oil baron."

"Was? As in past tense?"

"Yes, he died sometime last year. Huge funeral. I sold a lot of black Manolos that week. And speaking of Manolos," he said, checking his watch, "I've got to run or I'll be late for work."

"Aren't you going to finish your croissant?" I said, eyeing half a croissant on his plate.

"Nah, I'm full."

Leave it to a skinny person to be full after one and a half measly croissants.

Lance tootled off for work, and—after polishing off his croissant—I headed for the computer. I caught up on my parents' e-mails and groaned. Daddy was up to something, all right. One of these days, I swear, I'm going to see his mug shot on a post office wall. But I couldn't worry about Daddy. Not now, not with this murder hanging over my head. So I deleted all thoughts of my parents and logged on to the *L.A. Times* archives to do a search on Amanda Tucker.

Like Lance said, her name showed up in a bunch of society stories. One of the articles mentioned that she was the widow of the late billionaire Andre Tucker. Then I did a search on Andre, and guess what, folks? According to the *Times*, Andre died of food poisoning, leaving his wife his entire billion-dollar fortune. It was officially ruled an accidental death, but I wasn't so sure. After all, poison was poison. For all I knew, it was premeditated murder.

And just like that, I had a new Number-One Suspect.

Amanda Tucker lived in the toniest part of Brentwood, where fixer-uppers sell for millions. And Amanda's place was far from a fixer-upper. Separated from the street by a six-foot hedge, it had a front lawn as big as a football field. I parked my Corolla in the street, the only economy car for miles around, and began the trek up the path to the front door.

The house was an English country extravaganza, with leaded-glass windows and wood beams galore. I almost expected to see the Duke and Duchess of Windsor stroll out onto the front lawn for a game of croquet.

I'd decided to drop by unannounced and catch Mrs. Tucker by surprise. I figured she was less likely to turn me down if I showed up in person.

I rang the doorbell and sniffed the heady aroma of lilacs in bloom. The door was quickly opened by a stocky woman in a maid's uniform.

"Yes," she said, squinting at me. "What is it?"

I smiled my most engaging smile.

"I'm here to see Mrs. Tucker."

"If you're here about the Passions murder," she said, her arms crossed firmly in front of her formidable bosoms, "Mrs. Tucker has nothing to say except that Grace Lynbrook is one of the finest, most honorable women she's had the privilege to know."

She started to close the door.

"Wait," I said. "I'm not here about the murder."

"Oh? Then what do you want?"

I put on my tap shoes and started lying like a congressman up for reelection.

"Didn't they call you from the magazine?"

"No," she said. "What magazine?"

"*Vanity Fair.* We're doing a piece on Los Angeles fashion trendsetters, and we want to interview Mrs. Tucker."

"Nobody called from *Vanity Fair.*"

In the bright light of day, I could see a healthy mustache on her pursed lips.

"Damn those idiots at the office." I whipped out my cell phone and called my own answering machine.

"Kimberly," I barked into the phone, "I'm here at Amanda Tucker's and they say you never called to set up the appointment . . . I don't want to hear any excuses. You've got a job to do, so do it!"

I snapped the phone shut.

"Unbelievable!" I said. "These kids want to become writers, and they can't make a simple phone call."

The maid stared at me impassively. Was she buying any of this?

"Wait outside," she said finally. "I'll tell Mrs. Tucker you're here."

Whoopee! She bought it.

As I stood there cooling my heels, I realized I was taking a chance. After all, Mrs. Tucker had seen me at Passions. It was very possible she might recognize me. But I had the distinct impression that Amanda Tucker's main focus in life was Amanda Tucker. Somehow I didn't think she paid a lot of attention to the people around her. At least I hoped not.

Minutes later, the maid came back and nodded curtly.

"Follow me," she instructed.

And I did, to an English country living room, full of chintz and fresh-cut flowers. Amanda Tucker was waiting for me in tight white capri's and an even tighter pink angora sweater. I couldn't help noticing her boobs, two perfect globes, popping out from the angora. Manmade, no doubt.

"Pleased to meet you, Ms.—?"

"Russell," I said, improvising wildly. "Rosalind Russell."

Was I insane? Giving her the name of a dead movie star?

"You mean, like the movie star?"

"Yes," I smiled feebly. "My mom was a big fan."

"Have we met somewhere before? Your face looks familiar."

Damn. She was more observant than I'd thought.

"Possibly," I said. "Were you at the *Women's Wear Daily* cocktail thing last month?"

"No, that's not where I saw you."

"I have a very familiar face," I said. "This happens to me all the time."

"Oh, well. No matter," she said. "I'll think of it eventually. Won't you sit down, Ms. Russell? Can I have Gerta bring you something to drink?"

"No, I'm fine."

"Some apple strudel, perhaps? Fresh from the oven?"

"No, thanks."

Okay, so I didn't really say that. The words that popped out of my mouth, as you've probably already guessed, were:

"Sure. I'd love some."

Amanda momentarily abandoned her Lady of the Manor pose and hollered, "Gerta! Bring us some strudel."

Then she plopped her flat tush on the sofa opposite me and sat back against a small mountain of throw pillows.

"I'm just so thrilled," she gushed. "Imagine, being interviewed by *Vanity Fair*!"

Then she looked around.

"Where's the photographer? You are taking pictures, aren't you?"

"Of course. The photographer's coming later. That's how we work; I do the interview first, and then he comes to take pictures."

"Good," she said. "That will give me plenty of time to put on some makeup."

Yeah, right. As if she wasn't already wearing enough makeup to stock a Clinique counter.

"So," she said, plastering a smile on her taut face. "Fire away. Ask me anything."

What the heck was I going to ask her? I knew as much about high fashion as she did about Kmart specials.

"Um . . ." I finally managed, "who are your favorite designers?"

She started rattling off names and then suddenly stopped.

"Wait a minute. Aren't you going to take notes? Don't you have a tape recorder?"

"Right. My tape recorder."

I reached into my purse and took out my cell phone.

"Isn't that a cell phone?"

"It's also a tape recorder. Terrific little invention. The microphone is embedded right here." I pointed to one of the input holes at the end of the phone.

"What won't they think of next?" she said.

I put the phone on the coffee table.

"Try to talk into the little hole, okay?"

And she was off and running, rambling on about her favorite designers. It was then that I noticed the throw pillow she was cradling in her lap. It was moss green silk, embroidered with the motto *Don't Get Mad. Get Even.*

I remembered that day in Passions when Mrs. Tucker overheard Frenchie making fun of her and vowed she'd get revenge. I wondered if she'd made good on her threat with the help of a Jimmy Choo knockoff.

My musings came to a halt when Mrs. Tucker suddenly interrupted herself.

"Now I know where I saw you!" she cried. "Passions!"

Rats.

"Didn't I see you there, in a Prada suit?"

"That's right. I was there to interview Grace Lynbrook for my *Vanity Fair* story."

"That's funny," she said. "Grace never mentioned that you were interviewing her."

"That's because she signed our confidentiality agreement."

"Confidentiality agreement?"

"We make all our interview subjects sign a pledge to keep their interviews a secret until the story is actually published."

If I told one more lie, my nose would start growing.

"Besides," I said, "what with the murder at Ms. Lynbrook's store, I imagine our interview was the last thing on her mind."

Extra credit for me for steering the conversation to the murder.

"Terrible tragedy, wasn't it?" I said.

"Terrible," she echoed.

"Do you have any idea who might have done it?"

But I wasn't about to hear any of Amanda Tucker's ideas, because just then I looked out the window and saw Grace's Jaguar coming up the driveway.

I had to get the hell out of there, and fast.

"May I use your rest room?" I asked.

"Of course. It's down the hall to your right."

I tossed my cell phone in my purse and started for the door.

"Wait," Amanda said. "Why are you taking your tape recorder?"

"Battery's low. Gotta recharge."

I dashed down the hallway, bumping into Gerta, who was carrying a plate of warm apple strudel. Somehow I managed to restrain myself from grabbing a piece and continued down the hallway.

At last I found the bathroom, another floral fiesta

with hand-rolled linen guest towels and enough pot-pourri to fumigate the city dump. But its most important feature, as far as I was concerned, was a window. I quickly opened it and leaped out, landing in a lilac bush below.

(A word of advice: Try never to land in a lilac bush. They're not nearly as comfy as you might think.)

After extricating myself from the lilac branches, I crept along the side of the house until I heard Grace's voice coming from an open window. I stopped in my tracks and listened.

"Bad news," she was saying. "Some private eye knows that we were back at the store the night of the murder."

So I was right! They *were* at the store that night. Whatever they were up to, they were in it together.

"Not so loud," Amanda said. "The reporter might hear you."

"What reporter?"

"The one from *Vanity Fair*. She said she interviewed you for her story. On Los Angeles trendsetters."

"I didn't talk to any reporter from *Vanity Fair*."

"You didn't?" Amanda said, a most suspicious note in her voice.

I thought it was an opportune moment to make my getaway, which I did, plucking lilac twigs from my tush as I ran.

Chapter 18

I was back home in my bathroom rubbing aloe vera on my fanny when Becky called. She sounded excited.

"I just thought of something that could be really important," she said.

"What is it?"

"Well, this morning I went to the supermarket to get some carob powder to make brownies, and I accidentally locked myself out of my VW."

"And?"

"And when I looked in my wallet where I usually keep my spare key, the key wasn't there!"

So far, this sounded like a case for a locksmith.

"And then I remembered. A couple of months ago, Maxine's car was in the shop, and I loaned her my VW. I gave her my spare key. I forgot all about it, but today I realized she never gave it back."

"So, on the night of the murder, Maxine had a key to your car."

"That's right."

Very interesting.

"Do you park your car in a garage?" I asked.

"No, out on the street."

"Where Maxine would have had easy access to it. Which means she could've driven it to Passions."

Maybe R.D. Butler really did see an orange VW at the time of the murder. With Maxine the mousy accountant behind the wheel.

"It's so hard to picture Maxine as a killer," Becky said. "Besides, why would she want to implicate me? I never did anything to hurt her."

"To save her own hide."

"That's pretty rotten," Becky said.

"Killers usually are."

I hung up, promising Becky I'd have another chat with Maxine. Then I dusted my tush with baby powder and headed out to the valley. Putting my pants on first, of course.

I found Maxine and Sparkles watching *Breakfast at Tiffany's*.

"Jaine! How nice to see you," Maxine said, ushering me into her oatmeal living room. "It's the end of the movie, Sparkles' favorite part, where Holly Golightly rescues her cat."

Sparkles was curled up on Maxine's recliner, dead to the world, her tiny pink tongue hanging out from her mouth.

Maxine scooped her up in her arms.

"Wake up, Sparkles! This is the part where we always cry, remember?"

The three of us watched as Audrey Hepburn, George Peppard, and Audrey's orange cat embraced in the rain, and the credits rolled. Well, Maxine and I watched. Sparkles had conked out again.

"What a wonderful movie," Maxine said, with a sigh.

Then she clicked off the TV and turned to me, beaming.

"Guess what?" she said. "Grace has hired me back at Passions!"

"That's wonderful, Maxine."

"Why don't you stay for dinner and help me and Sparkles celebrate?" she said, shooting me a shy smile. "We're having Kentucky Fried Chicken. Extra crispy."

For a disgraceful instant I considered accepting her invitation. I happen to be particularly fond of the Colonel's cuisine. But I was about to accuse the woman of murder. I couldn't very well say, *Pass the wings, and by the way, did you bump off Frenchie?*

"Actually, Maxine, I came to ask you something about the murder."

"Oh?"

Was it my imagination, or did I see her stiffen?

"Becky says that several months ago, you borrowed her car."

"That's right. Mine was in the shop, and I had an important periodontal appointment. My gums were bleeding something awful. So Becky loaned me her car."

"Becky says you never gave her back her spare key."

"Oh, gosh. That's right. I forgot all about it," she said, jumping up from the recliner. "I'll go get it. It's got to be in my purse somewhere."

She scurried off and seconds later came back with a large brown tote.

"I carry so much junk in here," she said, rummaging through its contents. "Here it is. It was stuck in my pocket pack of Kleenex. I always carry Kleenex in my purse. And floss, too. One time I got a piece of shrimp stuck in my teeth; it was just awful. Ever since then I never leave home without floss in my purse.

"But I don't understand," she said, handing me the key. "What does this key have to do with Frenchie's murder?"

I took a deep breath. This wasn't going to be easy. I'd forgotten how fragile she was. Was I really going to accuse this little mouse of murder?

Then I steeled myself.

"Maxine, you didn't by any chance happen to drive Becky's car to Passions the night of the murder, did you?"

Much to my surprise, Maxine didn't fall apart. On the contrary, her face clouded over in anger.

"I already told you," she said, her jaw clenched. "I didn't kill Frenchie."

So. The mouse had some backbone, after all.

"What if I told you I had an eyewitness who saw a woman matching your description getting out of Becky's car that night?"

Now technically, I wasn't lying. I didn't actually say I *had* an eyewitness; I just asked her what she'd say if I had one.

"Whoever told you that is lying!" Her face flushed with anger. "I did *not* take Becky's car to Passions that night! I took my own!"

Then she gasped as she realized what she'd just blurted out. And suddenly, the anger was gone; the mouse was back. She looked scared to death.

"I think you'd better tell me about it," I said.

"If I do, will you tell the police?"

"Not unless it's absolutely necessary."

I sat there, trying my best to look trustworthy.

"All right," she said, finally.

She slumped down in the recliner and began stroking the comatose Sparkles.

"I couldn't sleep that night. I couldn't stop thinking

about how badly Frenchie had treated me. I decided to fix the account books, so she wouldn't be able to cheat Grace out of the store. At about two A.M., I drove over to Passions. But when I got there, Frenchie was already dead. I'll never forget that horrible sight as long as I live. I didn't stay to fix the books. I just ran. And that's the truth. I swear, I didn't kill her."

And then she burst into tears.

"You do believe me, don't you?"

"Yes," I said.

And at that moment, I did. But that didn't mean she wasn't a killer. Maybe all it meant was that I was a gullible softie and she was a damn good liar.

Then I handed her a Kleenex from her pocket pack and walked out the door.

Let's do a head count of all the people who showed up at Passions the night of the murder, shall we?

First there was Becky, who went back to get her designs. Then there were Grace and Amanda, who came to do Lord knows what. And now there was Maxine, who claimed she was there to re-cook the books. If any more people had shown up, they would've had to take a number.

I drove back home to Beverly Hills, making a pit stop at KFC. I'd had a craving for the Colonel's chicken ever since Maxine mentioned it. And I hadn't had a thing to eat since my croissants at breakfast, so I was starving.

Prozac sprang to attention when I walked through the door. That cat can smell chicken cooking in Nevada. She practically opened the bucket herself.

As she howled around my ankles, I cut up some bite-sized bits of chicken and put them in her bowl.

Then I settled down on the living room sofa with the bucket in my lap. I was just reaching for my second thigh when the phone rang. Remembering Prozac and the Case of the Purloined Roast Chicken, I took the bucket with me to answer the phone.

It was Kandi.

"So," she said, without any preamble, "what are you going to wear?"

"What am I going to wear where?"

"On your sunset cruise."

Damn. Today was my date with Darrell, the speed-dating sailor, and I'd forgotten all about it.

Kandi sighed theatrically. "You forgot all about it, didn't you?"

"Okay, so I forgot. Big deal."

"Yes, it *is* a big deal. How do you expect to wind up in a relationship if you can't even remember that you've got a date?"

"But I don't care if I wind up in a relationship."

"Of course you do. It's subliminal. You just don't realize it."

Now it was my turn to sigh. "I'm supposed to meet Darrell at the marina at four. It's almost three now. I'd better hang up and get ready."

"Good luck, sweetie. And wish me luck, too."

"Why? Where are you going?"

"On a date with Anton."

"Anton?"

"The New Age performance artist I met at Starbucks. He invited me to see his act."

"What does he do? Play Beethoven's Fifth on the espresso machine?"

"Très amusing, Jaine. I don't know what he does exactly. But whatever it is, I'm sure it'll be fantastic."

What can I tell you? Look up "optimist" in the dictionary, and there's a picture of Kandi. Look up "pessimist," and there's a picture of me. And just my luck, it'll be unflattering.

"This is so great," she said. "You're going out with your dream guy, and I'm going out with mine. It's like a spiritual double date."

"Kandi, how do you know he's your dream guy? You barely know him."

"I can tell. I've got an instinct for these things."

Yeah, right. When it comes to men, Kandi's instincts are about as reliable as a broken alarm clock.

"So aren't you going to wish me good luck?" she asked.

After wishing her gobs of good luck (something told me she was going to need it), I hung up and looked down into my bucket of golden fried chicken. I had a choice. I could either finish the bucket and show up for my date with a bloated tummy, or I could do the sensible thing and put the chicken in the refrigerator.

For once—alert the media!—I did the sensible thing. Honest. I put the bucket in the fridge. You can ask Prozac if you don't believe me.

I spent the next twenty minutes trying on outfits. I finally decided on jeans and a red T-shirt, topped off by a blue blazer and white sneakers. I was going for the natty-nautical look.

After brushing my teeth and gargling vigorously, I proceeded to slap on some makeup and blow out the curls from my bangs. I had no idea what the frizz factor would be like out at the marina, so I blasted my freshly straightened bangs with a helmet of hair spray. I threw the can of hair spray in my purse, just in case I ran into a passing fog bank.

My toilette complete, I said good-bye to Prozac, who was stretched out on the sofa, in a post-Colonel stupor.

"How do I look, Pro?" I said, twirling around for her approval.

She looked at me through slitted eyes.

Give me some more chicken, and I'll tell you you look great, was what I think she was trying to say.

"No more chicken for you, young lady. And don't try any funny stuff. I don't want to see any paw prints on the refrigerator when I come home."

Then I blew her a kiss and headed off for my date with Darrell, the speed-dating yachtsman.

Chapter 19

I tooled out to the marina in my nautical togs and enough hair spray on my head to poke a hole in the ozone layer. But as it turns out, I didn't need the hair spray. It was a glorious low-humidity day. Sometimes when it's glorious in Beverly Hills, it's Fog Central out by the water. But today it was magnificent all the way out to the beach.

I put a Cesaria Evora tape in my CD player and drove with the music blasting. Much to my surprise I was actually looking forward to this date. It felt good to get away from the murder for a while.

I parked at the slip where Darrell said he'd meet me. There was only one boat moored there. A fabulous yachtlike vessel, a symphony of gleaming wood and polished brass.

Did this floating bit of heaven actually belong to Darrell? Was my Bad Dating Karma finally about to be broken? Was this an end to the guys who brought calculators to dinner to split the bill? I suddenly felt an enormous surge of hope. Maybe Kandi was right. Maybe underneath it all, I really did want a relationship.

Then suddenly I heard someone call my name.

"Jaine!"

I looked at the yacht but there was no one in sight.

"Jaine! Over here."

I turned and saw a clunky gray hulk of a boat, with a Port of Los Angeles insignia on the side, pulling into the slip.

And there on deck was a muscular guy with close-cropped sandy hair who I vaguely recognized from speed dating.

"It's me! Darrell!" he said, waving eagerly.

Amazingly enough, he looked like a normal human being. Which just goes to show how you can't judge a book by its cover. Or in this case, a schnook by its cover.

"Ahoy, matey!" he shouted. "Welcome to *The Trashy Lady!*"

He hurried over to the railing to greet me.

"We call her *The Trashy Lady* because we patrol the harbor picking up garbage."

"You do what??"

"We pick up garbage. It's a garbage boat."

It looked like my Bad Dating Karma was alive and kicking.

"Actually, I just drove out to tell you I can't make our date. My cat's having emergency abdominal surgery."

That's what I should have said. But fool that I am, I just smiled and said, "Nice to meet you."

"Hop aboard!"

And he did mean hop. *The Trashy Lady* was surrounded by a three-foot-high railing. I stared at it, dismayed. The last time I'd done any serious hopping was in sixth-grade gym class. And even then, I wasn't very good at it.

"C'mon," he said. "Climb over."

Easy for him to say.

I spent the next few minutes with my fanny in the air, trying to hoist myself over that dratted railing.

"Let me help," he said, grabbing me by the waist.

"This is awfully embarrassing."

"Not a problem. I'm used to hauling heavy objects."

After depositing me on the deck like a beached walrus, Darrell introduced me to his partner, Bernie, a grizzly guy with a chewed-up cigar hanging from his mouth.

"It's just the two of us on the crew," Darrell explained. "Bernie mans the boat, and I rake in the garbage."

"Pleased to meetcha," Bernie said, chomping on his cigar. Then he shot me a pitying look and disappeared behind the controls.

Bernie revved up the motor, and seconds later, the *SS Trashy Lady* set sail amid the stench of rotting garbage.

"Smells pretty stinky, doesn't it?" Darrell grinned. "Sorry about that. After an hour or so, you'll get used to it."

Then he reached into a filthy knapsack. "I brought us refreshments."

He tossed me a can of Orange Crush and a package of peanut butter crackers.

Yum.

He broke open his package of crackers and started eating. The man had enough dirt under his fingernails to plant a rose garden.

"Say," he said, with a suggestive wink. "Want to see my tool?"

I wondered if I could possibly leap over the rail and swim back to shore.

Before I knew it, he'd whipped out his "tool," the rakelike contraption he used to collect trash.

"You'd be amazed at the stuff we pick up," he said.

Revolted was more like it. For the next two hours, I watched as Darrell used his "tool" to reel in a colorful assortment of condoms, inner tubes, abandoned underwear, and—the highlight of the voyage—a dead sewer rat. All the while, he regaled me with fascinating tales of *Amazingly Gross Stuff I've Found on My Job.*

"I'll never forget the time we towed in a bathtub with a decomposing body strapped inside. Wow, talk about stinking to high heaven. Phew! . . . Hey, how come you're not eating your crackers?"

"I'm not very hungry."

"You're not seasick, are you? Don't worry if you have to throw up. Most of my dates usually do."

After assuring him I was fit as a fiddle, Darrell resumed the saga of his life as a maritime garbageman.

"Of course, not everything I find is junk. I've picked up some very valuable items. Like a Barbie doll I once found. It was good as new, once I got the jellyfish out of her hair. I gave it to my niece. She loved it."

By now I realized Darrell didn't expect me to keep up my end of the conversation. He was perfectly happy reeling in trash and performing his monologue. So I just kept on nodding, like one of those stuffed animals with wobbly necks you see in the rear windows of cars.

"Hey, here's an interesting find," Darrell said, picking up something from the garbage hold. "A dead starfish."

I watched as he plucked a condom from one of its tentacles.

"Would you like to keep it? As a souvenir of our first date?"

"No, thanks. It's lovely, but my cat is allergic to starfish."

"You have a cat? I've got a pet, too. A snake. Betsy. I found her on garbage patrol. Poor thing was barely alive but I nursed her back to health."

And so it went, on and on for two mind-numbing hours. I just sat there, an idiotic grin plastered on my face, breathing in the bracing sea air laced with the scent of decomposing garbage. What more could a girl want?

It was toward the end of our cruise, when the sun was starting to set, when Darrell said, "Darn. I almost forgot. I brought you a pair of binoculars, so you could see the sights."

He handed me a pair of germ-ridden binoculars.

"Go ahead. Take a look. There's lots of interesting stuff to see on shore."

Praying I wouldn't catch some deadly eye disease, I began looking through the binoculars. On the plus side, at least I didn't have to look at the garbage.

"Look! Over there!" he said. "Behind the oil rigs. If you look really hard, you can see our sewage treatment plant."

I pretended to be engrossed in the scenery, trying hard to shut out the sound of Darrell's droning voice, when I saw a ship come into view—one of those dinner and dancing cruise ships that sail around the marina. I watched the lucky people on deck, laughing and sipping champagne, the sinking sun a glorious red ball behind them.

I was thinking about how life wasn't fair, and how I'd like to kill Kandi for getting me into this mess, when I saw something that grabbed my attention. There on deck, clinking champagne glasses with his date, was a guy who looked an awful lot like Tyler. I sharpened the focus on the binoculars.

It was indeed Tyler.

But the woman he was with wasn't Becky. It was a sweet-looking older woman with round apple cheeks and her hair caught up in a bun at the top of her head. It was hard to believe she was his date. Maybe it was his mother. How nice of Tyler, I thought, taking his mom on a dinner cruise.

But then, much to my amazement, Tyler put down his champagne glass and took the woman in his arms. He kissed her, a high-suction steamy lip lock. Whoever the woman was, it sure as hell wasn't his mommy.

The rest of my adventure on the high seas passed by in a blur. All I could think of was Tyler and his mystery woman. Before I knew it, we were back in the marina and Darrell was hoisting me over the rail onto terra firma.

"Thanks for a lovely time," I managed, with great effort, to say.

"My pleasure." Darrell smiled a big goofy grin.

Dear God, I prayed, please don't let him ask me out again.

"So, Jaine. How'd you like to get together sometime?"

"Well. . . ." I began, wondering if he'd believe me if I told him I was moving to Tasmania.

"Maybe I'll give you a call," he said, "once I work my way through my list."

"Your list?"

He nodded. "So far, I've lined up seventeen dates through speed dating. I want to see how the others go, and then maybe I'll call you."

It's nauseating, isn't it? Just think of all the wonderful women you know who can't land a date to save their souls. And guys with barnacles on their Barbie dolls are running around with lists.

Then Darrell winked and said, "Here's a little something to remember me by."

For a frightening instant I thought he was going to leap over the railing and kiss me. Or worse, show me his tool. But no, he just tossed me another package of peanut butter crackers.

Then he and Bernie went sailing off into the sunset. I didn't envy the sunset.

The first thing I did when I got home was head for the shower, to wash off the stench of that damn garbage boat. As I stood under the spray, I couldn't stop thinking about Tyler. Clearly he was cheating on Becky. But with who? Just who was that older woman I'd seen him kissing?

And then I remembered Tyler's alibi. He said he was with his writing professor at the time of Frenchie's death. He said her name was Ms. Garrett. Maybe Ms. Garrett was more than just a friendly advisor. Maybe she was also his lover, so much in love she'd be willing to give him an alibi for the night of the murder.

Chapter 20

The next morning, after a hearty breakfast of tap-water coffee and cold fried chicken, I drove over to the Westwood offices of UCLA Extension, home of hundreds of adult education courses.

Down in the lobby, I checked out the catalogue and found four courses in novel writing. One of them was taught by a Kate Garrett. Now all I had to do was find out if Kate was the same woman I'd seen smooching with Tyler.

I headed upstairs to the Writers' Program and approached the receptionist, an earnest young man with horn-rimmed glasses and eyelashes to die for.

"May I help you?" he asked, looking up from his copy of *How to Write a Screenplay in 21 Days*.

"I hope so," I said. "A friend of mine told me about a novel-writing course she took here. She said it was just fabulous. Unfortunately, I can't remember the name of the woman who taught it."

"All of our instructors are wonderful. You can't go wrong, no matter whom you choose."

Note the correct use of the word "whom." Obviously an ex–English major.

"I'm sure they are all wonderful," I said. "But I'〔
like to take the course my friend told me about. Sh〔
said the teacher was a sweet-looking woman, a littl〔
chubby, wears her hair in a bun."

"Oh, that must be Kate Garrett."

Bingo. So I was right. The woman on the boat *wa〕
Tyler's writing instructor. And it looked like Tyler wa〕
one hell of a teacher's pet.

"Her course is terrific. I can sign you up right now i〔
you give me your credit card."

I pretended to check my wallet, then slapped m〕
forehead in frustration. "Drat. I must have left it a〔
home."

He shot me a funny look. Maybe the forehead slap
ping was a bit over the top.

"If you're *really* interested in the course," he said〔
"you can register by phone. Or enroll on the Internet〕
All the information is on the back of the catalogue."

Then he lowered his incredible eyelashes and wen〔
back to finding out how to write a script in less tim〔
than it takes some people to get over the flu.

I hurried home and looked up Kate's name in th〔
phone book, but there was practically a whole page o〔
Garretts—no Kates—and I didn't feel like gettin〕
carpal tunnel syndrome from making phone calls al〔
day.

Then I had a brainstorm.

I called the UCLA payroll department.

The woman who answered sounded like she wa〔
counting the seconds till her coffee break.

"Payroll," she said, her voice oozing boredom〕
"Wanda speaking."

"Hi," I said. "My name is Kate Garrett. I'm an in〔
structor at UCLA Extension, and I haven't received m〕

last paycheck. It's way overdue, and I'm calling to make sure that you have my correct address."

"Social?" Wanda said.

"Huh?"

"What's your social security number?" she asked, with an impatient sigh.

Damn. It hadn't occurred to me that she might ask me that.

"Gee," I said. "My card's downstairs in the kitchen, and I'm up here in the bedroom. I sprained my ankle yesterday and it's so difficult for me to get down the steps. Can't you look me up by my name?"

"Oh, all right." Wanda sighed again. In the background, I could hear her tapping on her computer. "Here it is. Kate Garrett. We got you down at 1724 Glendon Avenue in Westwood, 90024."

"That's right," I said, frantically jotting down the address. "I don't understand why I didn't get the check. Probably some mistake at the post office."

I thanked Wanda profusely for her time and grabbed my car keys.

I was off to Westwood again.

Kate Garrett lived in a modest yellow stucco house not far from the university. She came to the door in a flowing batik caftan and wood bead necklace. With her round face and matronly bun, she looked like a beatnik Aunt Bea.

"Kate Garrett?" I asked.

"That's me," she said, smiling a warm Mayberry smile.

"I'd like to talk to you about Frenchie Ambrose's murder."

Suddenly, the smile vanished.

"Are you with the police?"

"No, I'm a private investigator."

"I'm afraid I can't talk right now," she said, finger-ing the beads around her neck. "I'm a writer, and I'm in the middle of a very difficult chapter."

She was about to close the door when I said, "Tyler's been cheating on you."

"What?"

"Your boyfriend, Tyler. He's been cheating on you."

The color drained from her cheeks.

"Tyler is seeing someone else?"

I nodded.

"Come in," she said.

I followed her into a small living room lined with bookshelves. I couldn't help noticing that there was a lot of Kate under that caftan. A far cry from Becky and her elfin figure.

She waved me to a seat on the sofa and sat down op-posite me in a large overstuffed armchair. Up close, she looked a lot younger than she had through Darrell's binoculars, but still, she had to be somewhere in her forties, way older than Tyler.

"How do you know about me and Tyler?"

"That's not important," I said. "The important thing is that he's been cheating on you with my client, Becky Kopek."

"Becky? He told me Becky was his cousin."

"And before Becky, he was having an affair with Frenchie Ambrose, the murder victim."

She reached into her caftan pocket and took out a pack of cigarettes. Her fingers shook as she lit one.

"How do I know you're telling me the truth?"

"Ask anyone at Passions. Ask the cops, for that mat-ter. They know."

If I'd expected her to melt down into a puddle of scorned womanhood, I was in for a surprise.

"I knew all along Tyler was too good to be true," she said, with a bitter laugh. "Why would a handsome young guy like him be interested in someone like me?"

She took a drag of her cigarette and let out the smoke with a sigh.

"He was using me, of course. Deep down, I knew it, but I couldn't admit it to myself."

"Using you?"

"It's been more than five years since my last book was published." She picked up a slim volume from the coffee table and handed it to me. "But I still have a lot of connections in publishing. Tyler was obviously willing to do anything to get his book published. Including sleeping with me."

I looked down at the author's picture on the back of the book and saw a younger version of Kate smiling that same sweet Mayberry smile.

"You can have it if you like," she said.

"That's awfully nice of you."

"Not really," she said. "I've got a hundred more out in the garage."

I guess it was safe to assume Kate never made it onto the best-seller lists.

"Did Tyler really stay after class the night of the murder?" I asked.

"For about five minutes. Just long enough to kiss me and tell me he loved me."

"So he could've been at Passions when Frenchie was killed?"

She nodded.

"The next day he called me, frantic. Told me Frenchie had been murdered. He told me how he'd threatened to kill her within earshot of a store full of customers. He was terrified the cops would arrest him. So I agreed to lie and say he was with me."

"If you keep lying to protect him, you could wind up in jail."

"Don't worry," she said. "I won't be lying for Tyler any more."

She stubbed out her cigarette with a vengeance, her eyes cold as ice. Bye-bye, Aunt Bea. Hello, Lady MacBeth.

Back home, I found a message from Becky on my machine. It was her day off, and she wanted me to stop by her apartment and give her a progress report.

I'm dying to know what happened when you talked to Maxine, her voice chirped from the machine. *For the first time, I'm beginning to feel like there's a ray of hope at the end of the tunnel.*

Oh, great. Just when she was hopeful, I was about to come along and stomp on her ray. What was I going to say to her? *Guess what, Becky? Your boyfriend doesn't have an alibi. And not only that, he's cheating on you.*

Reluctantly, I got in the Corolla and drove to Becky's place. She answered the door in hot pink tights and a lime green sweatshirt. With her Day-Glo orange hair, she looked like a technicolor test pattern.

Nina was lounging on the sofa in pajamas, reading the *National Enquirer.*

"Listen to this," she said, reading a headline. *"I Was the Love Child of Madonna and Tony Blair."*

"Who's Tony Blair?" Becky asked.

Nina shot her a reproving look. "Don't you know anything? He's the president of Canada."

I made a mental note to myself to never, under any

circumstances, wind up in a hospital with Nina as my nurse.

"I just made soy-carob-walnut brownies," Becky said. "You've got to try one."

She held out a plate of brownies. I say brownies advisedly. They looked more like bite-sized pieces of roofing tar. I smiled weakly and took one.

"Watch out for the walnuts," Nina said. "They can get caught in your esophagus and you can choke to death."

Becky bit into her brownie, ignoring the esophagus warning.

"So tell me about your visit with Maxine," she said, chewing happily.

I told her how Maxine had cheated and lied for Frenchie, only to have Frenchie dump her in the end, and how she'd driven to Passions the night of the murder.

"So she had motive and opportunity," Nina said, abandoning the bedroom antics of Madonna and Tony Blair.

"Yes, but she swears Frenchie was already dead when she got there."

"Big deal," Nina said. "She could be lying."

"Actually, Maxine wasn't the only one at the store that night. Grace and Amanda Tucker were there, too."

I told them what I'd overheard outside Amanda's living room window.

"Gosh, Jaine," Becky said. "You've done such a good job! You're just as good as any real detective."

I smiled stiffly, wondering if she was ever going to promote me to "real" detective status.

"I've got to pay you for all your time," she said, jumping up. "I'll go get my checkbook."

"Wait. There's something else you should know."

"What?" she asked, her blue eyes round and trusting, no idea of the ax that was about to fall.

"It's about Tyler."

"What about him?"

"For starters," I said, "he doesn't have an alibi."

"Of course he does. He was with his writing instructor when Frenchie was killed."

"I'm afraid not. I spoke with Tyler's instructor today. She told me she lied to cover for him. She said he left class that night with plenty of time to drive over to Passions and kill Frenchie."

"I don't understand," Becky said, scratching her orange spikes. "Why would she lie for him?"

Okay, here was the tough part. I took a deep breath.

"She was having an affair with him."

Nina gasped.

"That's not true," Becky said, shaking her head so hard I was afraid she'd sprain her neck. "She's making it up. Tyler told me she had a crush on him, that she kept coming on to him. But Tyler wasn't interested in her. She was way too old for him. He couldn't have liked her."

"I saw him kissing her, Becky."

She shook her head again, as if shaking it could somehow make me and my bad news disappear.

"I don't know where he told you he was last night," I said, "but he was on a dinner cruise in the marina. I saw him."

"No," Becky said, "that's impossible. It was somebody else you saw. Tyler would never cheat on me."

She raised her chin defiantly.

"I think you'd better go now. I don't want you working on the case any more. I'll send you a check in the morning."

Then, bursting into tears, she ran down the hallway to her bedroom.

"Damn," Nina said, shaking her head in dismay. "And I thought Tyler was such a nice guy. Men. What shitheels, huh?"

Then she tossed aside her *Enquirer* and hurried off to comfort Becky, whose sobs I could hear all the way from the bedroom.

Chapter 21

"So tell me all about your date. I want to hear every detail."

Kandi and I were having an early dinner at the Hamburger Hamlet, an upscale burger joint in Brentwood. We'd ordered bathtub-sized margaritas and were waiting for our bacon cheeseburgers.

"No," I said. "You don't want to hear every detail. Not without a barf bag."

I took a healthy slug of my margarita, licking the salt from the rim of the glass.

"Oh?" Kandi said. "It wasn't good?"

"Are you kidding? Try Utter Fiasco, Nautical Nightmare, Speed Date from Hell."

I gave her the highlights (or, more accurately, the lowlights) of my maritime adventure.

Kandi blinked in amazement. "He took you out on a garbage boat? Fed you Orange Crush and peanut butter crackers? Gave you a dead starfish? And put you on a dating wait list?"

"Yes to all of the above."

She just sat there, shaking her head. Then finally she regained her powers of speech.

"So? Do you think he'll call?"

"Kandi!"

"Okay, okay. I just thought maybe you might want to give him another chance."

"Are you crazy? I wouldn't go out with him again if he were the last garbageman on earth."

She shot me an apologetic look. "I'm sorry, hon. If I hadn't changed your speed-dating questionnaire, this never would have happened. I feel totally responsible."

"You *are* totally responsible. I would be strangling you at this very second if I could reach across the table without spilling my margarita."

"So," she said, ending what had to be the shortest guilt trip in the history of man, "do you want to hear about my date with Anton, the performance artist?"

"Sure," I sighed, resigned to the inevitable. "Tell all."

"You're not going to believe this. You want to know what his act was? He sat on stage naked in a bathtub filled with hot fudge! While he sat there, he recited all thirty-one Baskin Robbins ice cream flavors. Then, for the finale, he sprayed himself with Reddi-Whip. He called it *Sundae in L.A.*"

Wow. And I thought my date was a disaster. I was just about to offer Kandi my condolences when she said, "Isn't that just so incredibly creative?"

Oh, God. She actually *liked* it. The little idiot had fallen in love again. I could see it in her eyes. She was already plotting out her future with Anton, mentally moving in with him and buying black satin sheets for their hip downtown loft.

If you ask me, some people shouldn't be allowed into the dating pool without a lifeguard.

Our bacon cheeseburgers came, and strangely enough, I wasn't very hungry. Becky's brownie was sitting in my stomach like a lead balloon, defying the laws of digestion. I was so stuffed, in fact, I could barely finish Kandi's onion rings.

I listened to Kandi blather on about Anton's artistic vision until we finally paid the check and headed out to the parking lot.

"Don't worry, hon," Kandi said when we got to our cars. "One of these days you're going to wind up with a special someone to share your life and your bed."

"I've already got a special someone to share my life and bed."

"Cats don't count."

She hugged me good-bye and drove off in her Miata, visions of hot-fudge sex dancing in her head.

I drove home, wondering how long it would take for Kandi's affair with the Hot Fudge King to self-destruct. I gave it two months, tops.

After parking the Corolla, carefully checking to make sure I wasn't in front of a driveway, I headed up the path to my apartment. By now that damn soy-carob-walnut brownie was permanently wedged somewhere in my intestines. But I didn't have time to contemplate my gastrointestinal woes, because just then, scaring the living daylights out of me, I heard someone shout:

"You interfering bitch!"

My heart raced as Tyler stepped out from the shadows. No longer boyish and charming, but seething with rage. The same rage I'd seen the day he'd attacked Frenchie.

"You've ruined everything," he said, the veins in his temples throbbing.

"That's not true," I said, pasting a sickly smile on my face. "I didn't ruin anything. Becky still loves you."

"I'm not talking about Becky. I'm talking about that cow Kate Garrett. She knows an important editor at Random House. She was going to get him to read my manuscript. And now she won't give me the time of day."

He stepped closer.

"Do you realize what I went through to make that connection? I practically threw up every time I had to kiss her. And it was all for nothing, because of you."

I looked down and saw him clenching and unclenching his fists.

Oh, God. What if he tried to strangle me like he'd tried to strangle Frenchie? But he never actually hurt Frenchie that day, I reminded myself. He'd just threatened to. But maybe the only reason he didn't go through with it was because he knew there were a bunch of witnesses around. There were no witnesses now, though. Nothing to stop him from putting his hands around my neck and—

"Jaine? Are you okay?"

I turned and saw Lance standing in his doorway. Dear, sweet, nosy Lance!

"No, Lance. I'm not okay. Call 911."

Tyler blinked in the light from Lance's open door.

"Is that Tyler?" Lance asked. "The guy from Passions?"

"Yes, it's Tyler. Now call the cops."

"Oh, hi, Tyler," Lance said, with a friendly, flirty smile.

"For crying out loud, Lance. He's about to attack me. Will you please stop flirting and call the cops?"

Maybe Lance saw Tyler's veins throbbing like congas, or maybe he was cowed by the anger in my voice. Whatever the reason, he decided to take me seriously.

"Right, Jaine," he said, and disappeared back into his apartment.

But the threat of the cops showing up didn't seem to faze Tyler. He kept walking toward me, until he was so close I could practically scrape the tartar off his teeth.

"Don't come any closer," I said. "Or—"

"Or what?" he said, tauntingly. "What will you do?"

Frantically I searched my purse for something to hit him with. But as luck would have it, I was fresh out of blunt instruments. And then I came across the can of hair spray I'd tossed in my purse yesterday on my way to the marina.

I whipped it out with a flourish.

"I've got mace," I said, trying to hold the can so the label didn't show.

"It's not mace," Tyler sneered. "It's Extra Hold Spray Net."

I spritzed it anyway.

And guess what? It worked. As you probably know if you've ever had poor aim in a grooming session, the stuff stings like the dickens.

While Tyler covered his eyes and let out a string of curses, I took advantage of the moment and bolted into my apartment. Then, peeking out the living room window, I watched as Tyler staggered down the pathway out to the street.

By the time the cops came five minutes later, Tyler was long gone. This was the second time in two days the police had shown up on my doorstep. If I kept this up, they'd soon be naming a precinct after me.

I told the cops what happened, how Tyler had ambushed me and was going to attack me.

"I've got a witness. My neighbor saw everything."

I pointed to Lance, who'd hurried over to my apartment the minute Tyler had left.

The cops turned to Lance.

"You see him make any threatening moves?" one of them asked.

"Well . . . no."

"Did you hear him say anything threatening?"

"Not really. But he did look pretty angry."

"Last I heard," the cop said, "looking pretty angry isn't exactly a crime."

"I'm telling you," I said, my voice a hysterical shriek, "the man was going to attack me."

"Do you know where your alleged assailant lives?"

I didn't like his use of the word "alleged." Not one bit.

"Yes, as a matter of fact, I do." I dashed to my desk and rummaged through the drawer where I'd put the staff address list Becky had given me.

"Here it is," I said, handing it to the cops. "Tyler Benjamin. Third one down."

The cops wrote down his address, promising they'd question him and get back to me.

"You shouldn't be alone tonight," Lance said when they'd gone. "Why don't you stay at my place?"

"No, I'm fine."

"Are you sure?"

"Really. I'm fine."

But I didn't feel fine. Not even remotely. Which is why, the minute Lance trotted off to his apartment, I trotted off to my refrigerator for a snootful of chardonnay. My hands trembled as I poured some into a jelly glass.

Prozac, always acutely sensitive to my moments of stress, started yowling for a snack. I tossed her some Kitty Liver Treats and headed for the living room where I sunk down into the sofa.

After sipping (okay, gulping) my glass of chardonnay, I managed to relax a bit. My nerve endings had stopped doing their rendition of "Dueling Banjos," but I was still a far cry from calm. I kept seeing Tyler's hands clenching and unclenching, warming up for a strangling session. He was one seriously angry guy.

Angry enough, I felt certain, to have killed Frenchie Ambrose.

I made sure all my windows were locked, then got undressed and climbed into bed, clutching Prozac in one arm and the TV remote in the other. I was far too wired to sleep.

I was zapping around aimlessly, unable to focus on the screen, when I thought I heard a noise in the hallway. I bolted up in bed. Yes, I definitely heard something. It was the sound of breathing—loud, gasping breaths.

It had to be Tyler. But how had he managed to break in? I'd locked all the windows, hadn't I? Oh, God. Maybe he had some kind of special burglary tool that broke window locks with a flick of the wrist. He'd probably been hiding in the bushes all along, just waiting for the right moment to break into my apartment and strangle me.

My heart in my stomach, I was just reaching for the phone to call 911 when I looked over and saw that the heavy breathing was coming from the TV. I'd apparently zapped onto the Whoopsie Doodle Channel, where a couple of bad actors were writhing around on a waterbed.

I sank back down in bed, limp with relief. Really, if I ever wanted to be a success at this detective stuff, I had to stop being such a wimp.

I zapped away the sweaty lovers in favor of a nice

snooze-inducing infomercial on the benefits of coral calcium. Then, just when I finally managed to drift off to sleep, I was jolted awake by the sound of someone banging at my front door.

Oh, God. This time it really *was* Tyler.

I raced to the kitchen and grabbed the heaviest pan I could find so I could bop him over the head in case he forced his way in.

"Who is it?" I called out, in a trembling voice.

"Police."

I peeked out the living room window and saw the same two cops who'd come to the house earlier. I put down my frying pan and opened the door.

"Thank heavens it's you," I said.

"Hope we didn't wake you."

Heck, no. I always wander around my apartment at 2 A.M. clutching a frying pan.

"We spoke with Mr. Benjamin."

"Did you arrest him?"

"No, ma'am. We didn't."

"Why not?"

"He claims you invited him to your apartment."

"I did not!"

"He says you gave him your business card and told him he could contact you any time day or night."

Oh, damn. I *had* given him my card. That day we had lunch together at Pink's.

"Did you give him the card?"

"Yes, but—"

"Did you tell him he could contact you any time day or night?"

"Yes, but—"

"Mr. Benjamin claims you have a crush on him. And that when he wouldn't return your advances, you sprayed him in the eyes with Extra Hold Spray Net."

"That's a lie!"

"You didn't spray him in the eyes?"

"Yes, but—"

"With Extra Hold Spray Net?"

"Yes, but—"

Frankly, I was getting a little tired of my dialogue in this scene.

The cops exchanged glances. They clearly had me pegged as a hairspray-wielding spurned lover.

"You know, ma'am, you're lucky he didn't press charges."

Then they wished me a good evening and walked off into the night.

I trudged back to bed, where I found Prozac sprawled out on my pillow.

"That went well," I said, flopping into bed.

She looked up and meowed. Which was her way of saying, *As long as you're up, how about a snack?*

"Forget it, Pro," I said. I was in no mood to fix her a snack.

Which is why I spent the rest of the night sleeping without a pillow.

YOU'VE GOT MAIL

TAMPA TRIBUNE

LOCAL PLAY GETS DAMP RECEPTION

The Tampa Vistas Players' production of *Lord Worthington's Ascot* got off to a soggy start when an actor playing the part of a butler accidentally set fire to Lord Worthington's ascot and triggered the sprinkler system. No one was hurt, but theatergoers were soaked as they fled the Tampa Vistas Clubhouse.

"I knew all along that guy was a nutcase," said writer/director Alistair St. Germaine, referring to Tampa Vistas resident Hank Austen, who played the part of the butler.

Mr. Austen was unavailable for comment.

To: Jausten
From: Shoptillyoudrop
Subject: I Told You So!

I told you Daddy was up to something, and I was right. You're not going to believe this, but he set fire to the clubhouse! It's been the talk of Tampa Vistas. They even wrote about it in the *Tampa Tribune*. I've never been so humiliated in all my life!

I knew the minute the curtain went up there was going to be trouble. From his very first entrance, Daddy started mugging and winking at the audience. It was disgraceful. And the awful thing is, the audience loved it. They kept laughing at his silly antics, which just encouraged him. All the other actors were furious, but there was nothing we could do.

Then came the scene where Daddy was supposed to light Lord Worthington's cigarette. Daddy flicked on the lighter and, instead of looking at what he was doing, he turned and bowed to the audience. Naturally, he missed the cigarette by a mile, and wound up setting fire to Alistair's ascot instead! Alistair whipped it off and tried to stomp it out on the carpet, but then the carpet caught fire and the smoke triggered the sprinkler system. Up until then, the audience thought the fire was part of the play and were laughing like hyenas. But they didn't think it was so funny when the sprinklers went off. Everyone got drenched. Oh, honey. What a nightmare!

To: Jausten
From: DaddyO
Subject: It Was an Accident!

I suppose your mother has told you about the little incident at the clubhouse. Sweetheart, I swear it was an accident. You've got to believe me. I admit I was hamming it up, but I never intended to set fire to The Germ's ascot!

To: Jausten
From: Shoptillyoudrop
Subject: P.S.

I just got a call from the Tampa Vistas Board of Directors. Your father and I have been banned from the clubhouse for the next six months. Really, Jaine.

This is the last straw. I've had it with Daddy. I don't think I can ever forgive him.

To: Jausten
From: Shoptillyoudrop
Subject: P.P.S.

Guess what I just found next to my bowl of Cheerios? A diamond ring. All I can say is, if your father thinks I'm so shallow and materialistic that he can bribe his way back into my good graces with a diamond ring— he's absolutely right! I adore it. I hate to think what he spent on it. He bought it at a local jewelry store, though, so at least he didn't have to pay shipping and handling. And not only that, he's booked us on a cruise to the Bahamas. So I guess all's well that ends well. I never wanted to be an actress in the first place, and—more important—Daddy has given up his crazy dream of becoming an actor. For that I am truly grateful. From now on, I want to spend the rest of our lives out of the limelight.

To: Jausten
From: DaddyO
Subject: What a Hoot!

Hi, Sweetpea. Did Mom tell you? We're off to the Bahamas. It should be a lot of fun. They're having a talent show on the last night. I'm going to do a soliloquy from *Hamlet*. Either that or my Daffy Duck impersonation. Hey, wait. I know. I'll do Daffy Duck doing *Hamlet*. I think I'll rent a duck suit. What a hoot, huh? Don't tell Mom. I want to surprise her.

Chapter 22

I spent a ghastly night tossing and turning, jolting awake at the slightest noise, certain that Tyler was coming back to strangle me. I can't tell you how relieved I was when the sun finally came up and I was still alive.

I staggered to the kitchen for my morning cup of tap-water coffee. First thing, after my brain cells started functioning, I'd get dressed and pay a visit to Lt. Mula. I'd tell him about Tyler's social call last night. And how his alibi had been blown out of the water. I just hoped Mula would take me more seriously than the Beverly Hills cops.

By now all my other suspects had faded into the background. I was convinced it was Tyler who killed Frenchie. I'd bet my Prada suit on it.

After opening a can of Gourmet Chicken Gizzards for Prozac, I checked my e-mails and read the latest installment of my parents' adventures in the world of the theater. Can you believe it? Daddy actually set fire to the Tampa Vistas Clubhouse! And now he was about to unleash his Daffy Duck impression on a cruise ship full of unsuspecting passengers. Poor Mom. I only hoped she'd be so busy admiring her new diamond ring that she wouldn't mind Daddy running around in a duck suit. Oh, well. To paraphrase a famous philosopher: That which doesn't kill you really aggravates you.

I put a Pop Tart in the toaster and turned on the TV. Regis was doing a rant about a leaky faucet in his luxury condo when suddenly the show was interrupted by a Breaking News bulletin.

"This just in," said a bubble-haired newscaster, doing her best to look journalistic. *"Santa Monica resident Owen Ambrose was arrested early this morning and charged with the fatal stabbing of his wife."*

There, flashing on the screen behind Ms. Bubble Hair, was a photo of Owen.

"According to the authorities, Mr. Ambrose had taken out a two-million-dollar life insurance policy on his wife and had been involved in an extramarital affair with one of his neighbors, aspiring actress Tiffany Gustafson."

A picture of a brassy young blonde popped up on the screen. Something about her looked familiar. Where had I seen that face before? And then I remembered the twentysomething bimbettes I'd seen in the elevator of Owen's apartment building. She was one of the bimbettes. Good Lord. Was paunchy, middle-aged Owen having an affair with *her*?

I remembered how griefstricken he'd been that day, how the tears wouldn't stop. He seemed so damn pathetic. But maybe he wasn't pathetic. Maybe he was a sexy charmer who knew how to turn on the grief to fool a gullible writer/ detective. Everyone at Passions talked about how Frenchie cheated on Owen; it never occurred to anybody that Owen might have been cheating, too.

Now an on-the-scene reporter who looked barely old

enough to shave was standing outside police headquarters.

"Sources close to the investigation say that the suspect's fingerprints were found on the murder weapon and that traces of his wife's blood were found on an undisclosed article of his clothing."

The bubble-haired journalist in the studio thanked the pubescent reporter, and before I knew it, Regis was back on camera complaining about his in-laws.

I switched off the TV, dazed by what I'd just seen.

For a fleeting instant, I wondered if Owen could possibly be innocent. Not likely. Not with that two-million-dollar insurance policy and the bimbette lover waiting in the wings.

I had to face facts. I'd bungled this case badly. Five minutes ago, I'd been prepared to send Tyler to the electric chair. But I was wrong. Tyler wasn't a killer. He was simply a lying, cheating sociopath with an anger management problem.

So much for my skills as a detective. Oh, well. The important thing to remember was that Becky was in the clear. And the other important thing to remember was that my rent was due any day now, and I still hadn't lined up a writing assignment.

I'd have to buckle down and work on a promotional mailer. Today. Right now. This very minute. Well, maybe not this very minute. Maybe first I'd take a teeny tiny nap. What with Prozac stealing my pillow and me sitting up all night waiting for Tyler to strangle me, I was in terrible shape. I'd just lie down for ten minutes. . . .

Eight hours later, the phone jolted me awake.

"Cookie!" Mr. Goldman's voice came rasping over

the line. "You want to have dinner at the hospital with me tonight? We're having boiled chicken and creamed rice."

Just what I wanted, a bland food festival.

"Sounds mighty tempting, Mr. Goldman, but I don't think I can make it."

"That's okay, cookie. I understand."

I have to admit I was surprised. I thought for sure he'd give me a hard time.

"Of course," he said, "I wouldn't be here if you hadn't hollered at me, but that doesn't mean you have to have dinner with me."

Okay, so he *was* going to give me a hard time.

"I'll just have a lonely chicken breast all by myself," he sighed.

No way I was going to fall for this shameless guilt trip. I'd already pretended to be his girlfriend once: enough was enough.

"I was hoping you could cut my chicken for me. I haven't quite regained the strength in my right arm. But I'll manage somehow. Even though my wrist is weak as an egg noodle."

Oh, please. Give me a break.

"The doctor says I may never play Ping-Pong again."

Forget it. Nothing he said—absolutely nothing—would make me change my mind.

"We're having hot fudge sundaes for dessert."

"I'll be there in a half hour."

Dinner Chez Cedars was a delightful affair. You haven't lived till you've dined by the light of a heart monitor.

Mr. Goldman had managed to get the nurses to

bring two extra dinners, one for me, and one for Mr. Perez's girlfriend, Rosie. I pecked my way through dinner, cutting Mr. Goldman's boiled chicken, still going through the nauseating charade of being his girlfriend.

The dinner conversation went something like this (Diabetics beware!):

Mr. Goldman: *How's your boiled chicken, Honey Bunny?*

Me (with sickly smile): *Delish, Teddy Bear.*

Mr. Goldman: *Care for some salt substitute, Sweetums?*

Me: *No, thanks, Lambchop.*

I was counting the minutes till we finished our "hot fudge sundaes," which, incidentally, turned out to be nonfat yogurt with watery chocolate sauce.

Mr. Goldman: *How's your dessert, Honey Bunny?*

Me: *You lying son of a bitch, you promised me a hot fudge sundae!*

Okay, so I didn't really say that.

No, spineless wonder that I am, I said, "Yummy, Teddy Bear."

And if you think Mr. Goldman and I were nauseating, you should've seen Mr. Perez and Rosie. They kept tasting each other's food (for no apparent reason, since they were both eating the same thing), feeding each other with coy giggles.

"Say," Rosie said, winking at me. "When our fellas are better, the four of us should go out on a double date."

Oh, God. Spare me.

"Now if you folks will excuse me," Rosie said, hoisting herself up from her chair. "I got a piece of chicken stuck in my dentures. I'll be right back."

And then she hobbled off on her cane to the bathroom.

Mr. Perez smiled proudly. "She's some hot mama, huh, Goldman?"

"She's all right," Mr. Goldman said. "But she doesn't hold a candle to my Jaine."

Mr. Goldman patted my hand possessively.

"I gotta admit, you're right," Mr. Perez said. "Jaine's a pistol." Then he shot me a sly smile. "You know, maybe I should pull the plug on Abe, and then I'd have you all to myself."

What a prince, huh? Here he was, flirting with me when his girlfriend was in the very next room, picking food debris from her dentures.

After a few minutes, Rosie came hobbling out from the bathroom and gave us an update on the chicken-in-the-dentures crisis.

"I got it out," she said. "It was so big, I could've practically made a sandwich with it."

A tad more information than I needed to know.

"So," she said, patting her towering beehive hairdo, as if to make sure it was still there, "who wants to play Strip Parcheesi?"

Not me. Not in this lifetime.

"I do!" Mr. Goldman said, smiling at me eagerly. "How about it, Sweetums?"

"Actually, I've got to go."

"Oh, no. Really?"

"Yes, my cat's not feeling well and I've got to take her to the vet."

Mr. Goldman shot me a look.

"Wasn't she sick just the other day?"

"No, that was me. I had the emergency root canal. Remember?"

"Oh, all right," Mr. Goldman said, with a martyred sigh. "You go ahead. I don't mind being alone even though I'm awfully weak. Did I tell you the doctor said I may never play Ping-Pong again?"

"Yes, I believe you mentioned it, Teddy Bear, but I've really got to leave."

At this point, I didn't care if I *had* given him a heart attack; I positively refused to let him guilt me into a game of Strip Parcheesi.

And for once, I didn't weaken.

I blew him a kiss good-bye and sailed out of his hospital room, like an ex-con on her first day of freedom.

I was headed for the elevator when one of the nurses at the nursing station called out, "Excuse me, Miss!"

"Yes?" I said.

"Can I ask you a question?"

"Sure," I said, walking up to the counter.

The nurse who'd called me over, a plump young woman in pastel pink scrubs, smiled awkwardly.

"I hope you don't mind," she said, "but we have a bet going."

"A bet? About what?"

"Are you really Mr. Goldman's girlfriend?"

"No, I'm not!"

I was prepared to keep up that ridiculous charade in front of Perez, but not in front of the Cedars nursing staff.

"I told you," she said to the other nurses. "No one in her right mind would be his girlfriend."

"I have not now or ever been Mr. Goldman's girlfriend. I'm his teacher."

"Still," said one of the nurses, an older woman with glasses dangling from a cord around her neck, "it's awfully nice of you to visit him. It means so much to him."

"It's the least I could do," I said, "seeing as I'm responsible for him being here."

"Responsible? How are you responsible?"

"I yelled at him in class one night and he keeled over. If it hadn't been for me, he'd never be here."

"That's not true," said the nurse in the pink scrubs. "The man was a heart attack waiting to happen. It was just a matter of time."

"Huh?"

"His arteries were clogged pretty badly. Apparently he was skipping out on his cardiologist appointments and hanging out in the coffee shop of the medical building, eating banana splits and flirting with the waitresses."

Arrrgh! Was Mr. Goldman impossible, or what? Here he had me blowing him kisses and cutting his boiled chicken when that damn heart attack had been his fault all along.

I felt like marching back into his room and poking holes in his IV tube. At the very least, I'd tell Mr. Perez the truth about our so-called relationship. But what good would that do? Besides, I might wind up giving Mr. Goldman another heart attack. And this time, it *would* be my fault.

No, I'd let him get away with his silly lie, but from now on, I wasn't going to tolerate any more of his nonsense in class. No more interruptions. No more outbursts. No more insensitive critiques of his fellow classmates.

I was stomping toward the elevator, lost in thoughts of my new regime at Shalom, when I passed a petite redhead who bore a vague resemblance to Debbie Reynolds.

That was another thing, I told myself. No longer would I allow Mr. Goldman to tell those insane stories about having love affairs with movie stars.

I was pressing the button for the elevator when I heard the redhead say to one of the nurses, "Hi, hon. Can you help me?"

That was odd. Not only did she look like Debbie Reynolds, but she sounded like her, too.

"Of course, Ms. Reynolds," the nurse replied. "What can we do for you?"

I darted back to the nurses' station for a better look. Yikes, it really *was* Debbie Reynolds. Could it be? Had Mr. Goldman been telling the truth about his affair with the star of *Singin' in the Rain*? Nah. No way. Just because she was here at Cedars didn't mean she was going to visit Mr. Goldman.

"Which way to Abe Goldman's room?" she asked.

Okay, so maybe he knew her somehow. Maybe he once sold her wall-to-wall carpeting. That didn't mean they'd been lovers.

But then I heard her say, as she walked into his room:

"Abe, loverboy. How're they hanging?"

You could've knocked me over with a boiled chicken.

Chapter 23

I headed up the path to my apartment, my mind still reeling at the thought of Mr. Goldman and Debbie Reynolds as lovers. Had all his tales of romantic conquests been true? Had he actually, as he'd proudly claimed, danced the cha-cha with Ann-Margret, spent the night at the Disneyland Hotel with Joan Collins, and given Angie Dickinson a hickey?

Lost in thoughts of Mr. Goldman's love life, I opened the front door and almost tripped over something on my doorstep. A frisson of fear ran down my spine as I looked down and saw what it was: A shoe. A high-heeled, high-fashion number. Exactly like the one I'd found impaled in Frenchie's neck.

With trembling hands, I picked it up. The label said Jimmy Choo. Maybe it was real. Maybe it was a knock-off. But at that moment, I didn't much care about its authenticity. My attention was riveted to a Post-it stuck to the dagger-like heel. Written on it was a message, two little words that turned my frisson of fear into a full-blown panic attack:

You're Next

It had to be from the murderer. And yet, they'd ar
rested Owen this morning. So he couldn't have sent it
Was it possible the cops had arrested the wrong man?

True, Owen's two-million-dollar life insuranc
policy looked bad, but maybe Frenchie had a polic
out on his life, too. Lots of husbands and wives too
out mutually beneficial life insurance policies.

But if Owen was innocent, why were his fingerprint
on the murder weapon? Maybe after Frenchie had bee
gone several hours, he drove over to Passions to chec
up on her. Maybe she was already dead when he go
there. Perhaps he'd been foolish enough to touch th
shoe and get blood on his clothing. And then he pan
icked and ran out of the store, leaving a trail of incrim
inating evidence behind him.

The more I thought about it, the more I was con
vinced that the real killer was still at large. And tha
killer, I was certain, was Tyler. He had to be the on
who left Jimmy Choo on my doorstep.

My hands still shaking, I put the shoe and the Post-
in a plastic grocery bag. I wanted to preserve as man
fingerprints as possible. Then I got back in my Coroll
and drove to Lt. Mula's precinct. Mula was gone when
got there, so I left my package with the desk sergear
along with an urgent message for Mula to get back t
me as soon as possible.

I decided to swing by Becky's apartment on my wa
home. I had to get Becky to see how dangerous Tyle
was. Somehow I'd force her to listen to me. I'd tell he
how he'd ambushed me at my apartment last night, an
get her to accept the fact that he didn't have an alibi fo
the night of the murder.

I found a parking spot across from Becky's buildin
and was just about to get out of my car, when I looke
up and saw Becky's roommate, Nina, leaving for work i

her nurse's uniform, her cute little pageboy bouncing as she walked.

I started to wave to her, then stopped. There was something about her that wasn't quite right. And then I realized what it was. Nina was wearing a nurse's dress. Hardly any nurses wore dresses any more. Hadn't I just seen those nurses at Cedars all wearing scrubs? What's more, Nina's dress was awfully short—halfway up her thighs—and tight, too. Way too tight to change a bedpan.

By now, she'd crossed the street to her car, a beat-up old Camaro. And then she did something very strange. She opened the trunk of her car and took out a pair of stiletto heels. I flinched at the sight of them. If I never saw another pair of high heels in my life, I'd be a happy woman. I watched as she slipped them on and tossed her thick-soled nurse's shoes into the trunk.

What the heck was that about?

Up to then, I'd never connected Nina with the murder. But something in my gut told me I'd stumbled onto something important. So I decided to follow her.

Now I don't know if you've ever tailed someone, but trust me, it's not easy. Especially if the person you're following drives like a stunt driver on uppers. Somehow I managed to keep up with Nina as she zoomed across town to a seedy street on the fringes of Hollywood. I'm just glad there were no traffic cops around; otherwise I'd be doing five to ten in traffic school.

Eventually she turned into the parking lot of a strip club.

I could tell it was a strip club by the subtle neon sign flashing: NUDE GIRLS! NUDE GIRLS! NUDE GIRLS!

I pulled into a spot across the street and waited till I saw her go into the club.

Could it be? Was Nina actually a stripper? I got out of my car and crossed the street to The Frolic Room, as the club was called. There out front in a glass display case were eight-by-ten glossies of the club's "NUDE GIRLS!"

I scanned the photos of Lacy Garter, Patty Melt, and Fatima, the Islamabadgirl. But the photo I was most interested in was that of "Nurse Nina," wearing nothing but a G-string and a stethoscope.

Nina was a stripper, all right. But that didn't mean she had anything to do with the murder. She didn't even know Frenchie. Or did she? Was it possible that Frenchie had once worked here? I could easily picture Frenchie whipping it all off for a bunch of leering men. Maybe Nina had known Frenchie. And as we all know by now, to know Frenchie was to loathe her. So maybe Nina had a reason to kill her, after all.

I needed to find out. I put on my sunglasses and an old baseball cap I kept in the trunk of my car for emergency bad hair days and headed in to The Frolic Room.

I was happy to see that it was dark inside and that Nina was nowhere in sight. I sat down at a table way in back. Nina would never be able to see me past the bright stage lights.

The place was fairly empty, just a few glassy-eyed guys staring at Lacy Garter, who was up on stage doing obscene things with a black lace garter. One or two of the men shot me covert glances, but most of them were too busy frolicking with themselves under the table to pay much attention to me.

A weary waitress in hot pants and what looked like a black leather bra came sidling up to the table. Under her thick makeup I could see she had bad skin.

"What'll it be?" she asked, tossing a wilted cocktail napkin on the table.

Frankly, I was hungry. That boiled chicken extravaganza at Cedars wasn't exactly filling.

"Got any pretzels? Or peanuts?"

She looked at me as if I'd just stepped off Planet Idiot.

"You want pretzels," she snapped, "there's a 7-11 down the street. Now what'll you have *to drink*?"

"A Coke."

"It's ten dollars."

"Ten dollars for a Coke?"

"Plus a two-drink minimum."

Geez. What some horny men won't pay to see a woman take off her garters. I was tempted to leave, but I needed to find out if Frenchie had ever worked there.

"Great," I said. "Bring me two ten-dollar Cokes."

She nodded curtly and walked off.

By now, Lacy had both garters dangling from her boobs and was twirling them around like miniature hula hoops. I have to admit, it was really quite impressive.

My friend the waitress came back and plopped two large Cokes on the table.

"You sure you're in the right place?" she asked. "There's a lesbo club a few blocks away, right next to the 7-11."

A real fount of information, wasn't she?

"Actually," I said, "I'm looking for a friend of mine who used to work here. Name of Giselle Ambrose. Everybody called her Frenchie. You ever hear of her?"

"Sure."

Bingo. My hunch was right.

"She's the one who got iced with a shoe," she said. "I saw it on the news."

"Did she ever work here?"

"Nope. At least I've never seen her, and I've been here fifteen years."

So much for my hunches.

She sashayed back to the bar and I eyed my Cokes unhappily. Twenty bucks down the drain, and for nothing. Nina hadn't known Frenchie. The most she was guilty of was lying to her roommate about being a stripper.

Oh, well. I'd finish these damn Cokes if it killed me.

So, as Lacy wound up her act and Fatima the Islamabadgirl slinked onstage with a sequinned veil over her crotch, I started sucking my Cokes. By the time I'd worked my way through both of them, I had to pee. Big time.

Great. Now I'd have to use The Frolic Room's john. I could just imagine how filthy it would be. Why hadn't I just paid the twenty dollars and taken a loss on the Cokes?

I asked the waitress where the ladies' room was, and she pointed down a dank hallway.

True to my expectations, the bathroom was a nightmare. It had fungus on the walls left over from the Eisenhower administration. Think Black Hole of Calcutta, with Tampax machines.

I pulled down my jeans and crouched over the toilet, trying desperately not to come into contact with any disease-ridden surface. I used a paper towel to turn on the hot water to wash my hands, and another one to open the door back out to the hallway. I swear, you practically needed a vaccination to take a tinkle in that joint.

When I got back to my table, I waved to the waitress to get my check. She came over with a martini and a basket of fries that smelled pretty darn delicious. I eyed them hungrily.

"I thought you said you didn't have food."

"I said we didn't have *pretzels*. I didn't say nothing about fries."

"It doesn't matter," I said. "I didn't order this stuff."

"I know. It's from that guy over there."

She nodded in the direction of a boozy old guy with a big gut and wet lips who shot me a sloppy grin.

Now if I'd had any sense I would've cleared out right then and there. The last thing I needed was an order of fries. But I was hungry. And those fries looked great. I'd just have one or two, and then I'd go.

Before I knew it, I was chomping through the whole basket of fries, washing them down with the martini. I tried to avoid making eye contact with the leering old fart who'd sent them to me. The guy was easily in his sixties. He should've been home taking his Metamucil, not hanging out in a dive like this. What was it with me and old farts, anyway? First Mr. Goldman. And then Mr. Perez, hitting on me with his girlfriend in the next room. I remembered what Mr. Perez said about pulling the plug on Mr. Goldman so I'd be free to date him.

And that's when it hit me. That's when I knew that Nina was the killer.

True, Nina didn't know Frenchie. But maybe she didn't care about Frenchie. Maybe the person she wanted to get rid of was Becky.

Maybe Nina had fallen for Tyler, and fallen for him hard. I remembered how her eyes shone when she first told me what a great guy he was. Maybe she came on to him, but he was too wrapped up with Becky to give her a tumble. So she decided to get rid of her competition. Maybe, like Mr. Perez, she simply wanted her rival out of the way.

And so when Becky came home one night and told her about her fight with Frenchie, and how she said—

in front of a store full of customers—that she'd like to see Frenchie's corpse on the sales floor, Nina got an idea. She spotted Becky's earring, which Becky had dropped—not at Passions—but somewhere in the apartment. She pocketed the earring and pretended she couldn't find it when she and Becky searched for it. She didn't go to work that night. Instead, she lured Frenchie to the shop with a phony call about a burglary. Then she bumped her off, carefully planting Becky's earring at the scene of the crime.

What better way to get rid of her rival than getting her arrested for murder?

Of course, it was all just a theory. I had no proof. None whatsoever.

By now Fatima had removed her last veil and was undulating offstage. I wanted to be gone when Nina showed up for her act. So I plunked down some cash and got up to leave. The old coot who'd sent me the drink was motioning me to his table, but I hurried past him and made my way outside.

God, I was loaded. That was one hell of a stiff martini. I headed across the street to my Corolla, sucking in the cool night air, trying to sober up. But by the time I reached my car, my head was spinning and my legs were as wobbly as Jell-O. There was no way I was driving home like this. I'd simply have to call a taxi.

I opened my purse to get my cell phone, and then everything went black as the fungus on The Frolic Room's toilet.

Chapter 24

I woke up in Grace's office at Passions, my head pounding with a killer headache. It felt like Desi Arnaz was playing "Babaloo" on my cranium.

The first thing I saw when I opened my eyes was Nina standing over me. The second thing I saw was a gun in her hand, aimed straight at my heart.

Then I glanced to my side and saw a disembodied arm on the floor beside me. I flashed on Nina's fondness for medical horror stories. Oh, God. She was probably one of those wackos who got their jollies out of cutting people up into bite-sized pieces. The demented psychopath had amputated my arm!

"What have you done to my arm?" I shrieked.

"What're you talking about? I haven't touched your arm."

Then I looked over and saw Bessie the mannequin propped up against the wall. It was Bessie's arm lying next to me, not mine. What a relief. At least now I'd have all my limbs when Nina killed me.

"How did you know I was at the club?" I asked.

"I saw you following me in your car. You were so

close I could see your face in my rearview mirror. The next time you tail someone, keep your distance.

"Not that there's going to be a next time," she said, waving the gun.

She stood straddled over me, giving me an X-rated view up her short nurse's dress.

"It didn't have to come to this," she said. "I tried to warn you."

"By leaving that Jimmy Choo on my doorstep?"

"I went to a lot of trouble to steal that shoe," she said, looking rather miffed, "but did you pay attention? Noooo. And now look at you. You should've minded your own business."

Truer words were never spoken, I thought, gazing up her crotch.

"Hey," she said, brightening, "it's too bad you didn't get a chance to see my act."

And with that, she whipped off her uniform. It was one of those breakaway costumes designed to come off at the slightest tug.

"What do you think?" She smiled down at me, naked except for a sequinned G-string and pasties.

Good Lord. In addition to being a crazed psychopath, she was also a world-class narcissist.

"I've got a great body, don't I?" she said, stroking her hips.

I'd always thought of Nina as a delicate little thing. But now I was surprised to see that her body was roped with well-defined muscles. She sure looked a lot tougher without her clothes on.

"Not an ounce of fat anywhere," she preened. "Not like you, Jaine. You gotta do something about those thighs, honey."

Just what I wanted. A pre-execution diet lecture.

"I read somewhere that the cellulite from your thighs can travel to your brain and cause cancer."

Where did she get this stuff? The Abbott & Costello School of Medicine?

"It's a proven fact. The more you weigh, the younger you die. And that's certainly going to be true in your case," she said, once again waving that damn gun in my face.

By now I was getting mighty tired of looking up her crotch.

"Is it okay if I sit up?"

"Sure, why not?"

I sat up, setting off a fresh wave of bongos in my brain.

"What did you do?" I asked. "Slip something in my drink?"

"While you were in the bathroom," she nodded. "Knockout drops. I use 'em to roll my tricks."

"Your tricks? You're a hooker, too?"

"Hey," she shrugged. "A gal's gotta make a living."

"Does Becky know about any of this?"

"Are you kidding?" she sneered. "She's the original clueless wonder. It's amazing, isn't it, how men fall for stupid women? Becky just smiles that dopey smile of hers, and they're in love. I don't get it. I'm smarter than her. And prettier, too. And they never choose me."

Perhaps because they sense you're a raving nutcase, were the words I wish I could have uttered.

"Up till now, I didn't mind," she said. "Because all the guys Becky dated were losers. But Tyler, he was something else. The first time I laid eyes on him, I knew I had to have him. But all he could see was Becky. Life sure isn't fair, is it?"

I had to agree with her on that one.

"So you figured out a way to get rid of her," I said. "You decided to get her arrested for murder."

"Clever of me, wasn't it? Killing somebody I didn't even know. That way, the cops would never suspect me."

She was so damn proud of herself, she was practically strutting.

"I bought a gun, then lured Frenchie to the store, pretending to be from the alarm company. I told her it was nothing personal but I had to blow her brains out. But when I pulled the trigger, nothing happened. Can you believe it? The crack dealer who sold me the gun didn't tell me there weren't any bullets in it. What a bummer, huh?"

Yep, those darn crack dealers. They're so unreliable.

"The minute Frenchie realized the gun wasn't loaded, she made a break for it. She almost got away but she tripped and went splat on the floor. I tackled her from behind. Then I saw her Jimmy Choo and decided it would make a dandy murder weapon. And guess what? I was right."

Another smug smile.

"And after you killed her," I said, "you planted Becky's earring in her hand."

"Becky was always losing that stupid earring. She'd dropped it at the apartment that night, and I picked it up when she wasn't looking. Then after she went to sleep, I took her car and met Frenchie at the shop."

So the musician next door really did see Becky's car in the parking lot at the time of the murder.

"I watched as Frenchie disarmed the alarm system, and I memorized the code. That's how I was able to get us in here tonight. Pretty smart, huh? When they find your body, they'll think it was an inside job. Only someone who works here would know how to disarm the alarm.

"And when they find these all over you," she added, taking a plastic baggie from her purse, "they'll be convinced Becky did it."

She tossed me the baggie. Inside were some bright orange hairs.

"I got 'em off Becky's hairbrush. Rub them on your clothes, will ya?"

Reluctantly, I obeyed instructions.

"If this doesn't get the little idiot arrested, I'll have to shoot her myself. Which reminds me. It's time to say bye-bye, Jaine. And this time, the gun is loaded."

She raised the gun and took aim.

Oh, God. This was it. My final moment on earth. And my last sight was a nutcase in a G-string and pasties. I had to think of something—anything—to get her to put down the gun.

"You realize you're being taped, don't you?"

"What?"

For the first time since this little scenario began, she looked unsure of herself.

"After Frenchie got killed," I said, "Grace installed a security camera. It's right over there."

I pointed to the far wall. Of course, there was no security camera. But Nina didn't know that. She whirled around, and when she did, I grabbed Bessie's mannequin arm and whacked her in the legs as hard as I could. As she stumbled forward, I whacked her again, this time in the arm. Her gun went flying across the room. We both raced for it.

And in a gratifying moment of poetic justice, I watched as Nina tripped on her stilettos and went sprawling onto the floor, just as Frenchie had done right before Nina stabbed her in the jugular.

I grabbed the gun, and now it was Nina's turn to lie on the floor, staring up into the barrel of a lethal weapon.

"I'm sure the police will be very interested in our little chat," I said.

"Go ahead," she said. "Tell the cops. It's your word against mine. You have no proof that I killed Frenchie."

"Oh, yes, she does."

We turned and saw Maxine standing in the doorway.

"Hi, Jaine," she said, with a shy smile. "I stayed late to work on the books."

Thank God for workaholics.

"I heard everything," she said.

"Great," I said. "Now please call the cops."

"I already did."

As if on cue, we heard the faint wail of a police siren.

I looked down at Nina, whose eyes were blazing with fury.

"Fat people may die young," I said, "but people on death row die even younger."

Then I picked up one of her pasties, which had fallen off during our scuffle.

"Better put this back on," I said, tossing it to her. "You don't want to catch cold."

Epilogue

You'll be happy to know that Becky came to her senses and broke up with Tyler. She quit her job at Passions and moved down to Hermosa Beach, where she's now designing swimsuits for a local surf shop. They're in wild Day-Glo colors with daisies sewn in strategic places. She calls them Beckinis.

Needless to say, she's sworn off roommates forever.

What with all the publicity from Frenchie's murder, Passions has practically become a tourist attraction. Grace is still defying the laws of gravity and looking amazingly young. Maxine is still doing the books and going home at night to Sparkles—and her new kitty, Sparkles, Jr. And Amanda Tucker is still running around with enough botox in her face to paralyze the population of Peru.

(Not long ago, I bumped into Grace and Amanda at Amanda's alma mater—the Chanel counter at Bloomingdale's—and they finally confessed that they were indeed at Passions the night of the murder. Like Maxine, they went there to get the account books. And like Maxine, they panicked and ran at the sight of Frenchie with a Jimmy Choo in her neck.)

Wonderful news about Kate Garrett, the UCLA writing instructor. She sold another novel. About a middle-aged woman who has an affair with her scheming, amoral writing student. Something tells me this one won't wind up gathering dust in her garage.

And speaking of scheming, amoral writing students, last I heard, Tyler was writing spec scripts and dating an agent at ICM.

Believe it or not, Kandi's still dating Anton, the performance artist. I guess you can never underestimate the allure of a guy with hot fudge sauce in his ears.

As for me, I'm back in the land of T-shirts and elastic-waist pants. And wouldn't have it any other way. Although I really must drop a few pounds. Which is why I've started a strict new diet. Absolutely no carbs, low fat, and high protein. Aren't you proud of me?

The guys at Tip Top Dry Cleaners fired their ad agency and came groveling back to me, begging me to take their account again. Okay, so I did the groveling, but at least they're back, and I'm busy writing blockbuster slogans like *Free Pick-Up and Delivery*, and *We Specialize in Leather and Suede.*

And you'll never guess who I heard from the other day. Darrell, the speed-dating yachtsman. He worked his way through his list of seventeen women and was ready to give me a chance. I fibbed a bit and told him I was dating someone else and moving to another state, and had recently discovered I had latent lesbian tendencies. He seemed turned on by the lesbian stuff, so I managed to get off the phone by telling him I felt a seizure coming on.

Oh, and I've got good news and bad news about my Prada suit. The good news is: The cleaners got out the wine stains. The bad news: They lost the buttons.

Which is why I've got to get back to work and earn some money right now. And I will. Right after I feed Prozac and finish my donut.

Okay, so I lied about the diet.

Sometimes-sleuth Jaine Austen struggles to make ends —and zippers—meet while living on a freelance writer's salary in Los Angeles. When she's not hunting down the latest flavor of her favorite ice cream, she's tracking down criminals on her own Walk of Infamy . . .

On the frontlines of the battle of the bulge, otherwise known as trying on bathing suits in the communal dressing room at Loehmann's, Jaine makes a new friend—a wanna-be actress named Pam—and gets a new job: sprucing up Pam's barebones résumé. Their feeling of connection is mutual, so Pam invites Jaine to join The PMS Club—a women's support group that meets once a week over guacamole and margaritas to commiserate about love and life.

But joining the club proves to be more of a curse than a blessing for Jaine. Though she is warned that Rochelle, the hostess, makes a guacamole to die for, Jaine never takes the warning literally. Until another PMS member—Marybeth, a relentlessly perky interior decorator—drops dead over a mouthful of the green stuff after confessing she is having an affair with Rochelle's husband. Turns out that someone knew about Marybeth's nut allergy and added a fatal dose of peanut oil to the dip.

While Rochelle and her husband are the obvious suspects, everyone at that night's meeting is under suspicion, including Jaine, putting a new job opportunity at a conservative downtown bank in jeopardy. So, instead of dishing dirt with The PMS Club, Jaine has to dig up dirt on the surviving members—an alcoholic widow, a sassy sixty-something, a too-fabulous honorary male PMS-er, and Pam. As Jaine delves deeper, she tunes into some truly sinister vibes, and it soon becomes clear: someone in this club thinks getting away with murder should be a privilege of membership . . .

Please turn the page for an exciting sneak peek at
The PMS Murder
coming next month!

Chapter 1

What's more painful than a mammogram? More excruciating than a bikini wax? More humiliating than spinach stuck to your front tooth?

Shopping for a bathing suit, of course.

There's nothing worse. Not even a root canal. (Unless it's a root canal in a bathing suit with spinach stuck to your front tooth.)

That's what I was doing the day I first became involved in what eventually became known as the PMS Murder: trying on a bathing suit. For some ridiculous reason I'd decided to take up water aerobics. Actually, for two ridiculous reasons: my thighs. Before my horrified eyes, they were rapidly turning into Ramada Inns for cellulite.

So I figured I'd join a gym, and after a few weeks of sloshing around in the pool, I'd have the toned and silky thighs of my dreams. But before I could get toned and silky, there was just one tiny obstacle in my way: I needed to buy the aforementioned bathing suit.

I knew it would be bad. The last time I'd gone bathing suit shopping, I came home and spent the night crying on the shoulders of my good buddy José Cuervo. But I never dreamed it would be this bad.

For starters, I made the mistake of going to a discount clothing store called the Bargain Barn. My checkbook was going through a particularly anemic phase at the time, and I'd heard about what great prices this place had.

What I hadn't heard, however, was that there were no private dressing rooms at the Bargain Barn. That's right. Everyone, I saw to my dismay, had to change in one ghastly mirror-lined communal dressing room, under the pitiless glare of fluorescent lights, where every cellulite bump looked like a crater in the Grand Canyon.

It's bad enough having to look at your body flaws in a private dressing room, but to have them exposed in a roomful of other women—I still shudder at the memory.

Making matters worse was the fact that I was surrounded by skinny young things easing their washboard tummies into size twos and fours. I once read that sixty percent of American women are a size twelve or larger. Those sixty percent obviously didn't shop at the Bargain Barn. But I shouldn't have been surprised. After all, this was L.A., the liposuction capital of the world, where it's practically against the law to wear a size twelve or larger.

I grabbed a handful of bathing suits, ignoring the bikinis and mini-thongs in favor of the more matronly models with built-in bras and enough industrial-strength spandex to rein in a herd of cattle.

I jammed my body into one hideous swimsuit after another, wondering what had ever possessed me to come up with this insane water aerobics idea. I tried on striped suits and florals; tankinis and skirtinis; blousons and sarongs. No matter what the style, the end result was always the same: I looked like crap.

One suit promised it would take inches of ugly flab from my waist. And indeed it did. Trouble was, it shoved that ugly flab right down to my hips, which had all the flab they needed, thank you very much.

I'd just tried on the last of the bathing suits, a striped tankini that made me look like a pregnant convict, when suddenly I heard someone moaning in dismay.

I looked over and saw a plump thirtysomething woman struggling into a pair of spandex bike shorts and matching halter top. At last. Someone with actual hips and thighs and tummy. One of the sixty per-centers!

She surveyed herself in the mirror and sighed, her cheeks flushed from the exertion of tugging on all that spandex.

"My God," she sighed. "I look like the Pillsbury Doughboy with cleavage."

"Tell me about it," I said. "I look like the doughboy with cleavage, retaining water."

"Oh, yeah?" she countered. "I look like the dough-boy with cleavage, retaining water on a bad hair day."

She ran her fingers through her blunt-cut hair and grimaced.

"Would you believe this is a size large?" she said, tugging at the shorts. "Who is this large on? Barbie?"

"Well, I've had it." I wriggled out of the tankini and started to get dressed. "I'm outta here."

I'd long since given up my insane water aerobics idea. No. I'd take up something far less humiliating. Like walking. And the first place I intended to walk to was Ben & Jerry's for a restorative dose of Chunky Monkey.

"I'm going to drown my sorrows in ice cream."

"Great idea," said my fellow sufferer. "Mind if I join you?"

"Be my guest."

And so, ten minutes later, we were sitting across from each other at Ben & Jerry's slurping Chunky Monkey ice cream cones.

"I'm Pam, by the way," my companion said, licking some ice cream from where it had dribbled onto her wrist. "Pam Kenton."

It was nice being with someone who ate with gusto. My best friend Kandi has the appetite of a gnat and usually shoots me disapproving looks when I order anything more fattening than a celery stick. I know it's only because she cares about me and wants me to be one of the skinny forty percenters, but still, it can get pretty annoying.

"Actually," Pam said, "my last name isn't really Kenton. It's Koskovolis. Kenton is my stage name. I'm an actress. Of course, you know what that means in this town."

"Waitress?"

"You got it," she nodded. "And you?"

"I'm a writer."

"Really?" Her eyes widened, impressed. People are always impressed when I tell them I'm a writer. "What do you write?"

"Oh, industrial brochures. Résumés. Stuff like that."

Here's where they usually stop being impressed. Most folks find résumés and industrial brochures a bit of a yawn.

But Pam sat up, interested.

"You write résumés? I sure could use some help with mine. I'm getting tired of waitressing. I want a job where I get to sit down for a while."

"I'd be happy to help you with your résumé," I offered.

A worry line marred her brow. "I couldn't afford to pay you much."

"Oh, don't worry about the money. I won't charge you."

Inwardly, I kicked myself. What was wrong with me? Why was I always giving away my services? If I started charging people, maybe I wouldn't have to shop at joints like the Bargain Barn. Oh, well. Pam seemed awfully nice, and it wasn't as if I had a lot of assignments that she'd be interfering with. In fact, my work schedule was scarily light.

"That's so sweet of you," Pam said. "How about I fix you dinner as payment?"

"Sounds great. When do you want to get together?"

"As soon as you can."

"How about tomorrow night?"

"Oh, I can't tomorrow," she said. "That's PMS night."

"PMS night?"

"A group of friends get together once a week to bitch and moan over guacamole and margaritas. We call ourselves the PMS Club."

"Sounds like fun."

"Hey, wait. I've got a great idea. Why don't you come with me? We're short on members right now and I think you'd be a great addition to the club. We could have dinner first at my place while we work on my résumé and then head over to the club afterward. What do you say?"

"Are you sure the others won't mind?"

"No. They're going to love you; I'm sure of it. And it's really worthwhile. You get to share your innermost thoughts with like-minded women in a warm, supportive environment.

"Plus," she added, with a grin, "you get great guacamole and free margaritas."

"Sure," I said, never one to pass up a free margarita. "Why not?"

I was soon to find out exactly why not, but that's a whole other story. Stick around, and I'll tell it to you.